THE
LOST
KING

PEARSON

Heinemann

THE
LOST
KING

scot gardner

www.pearsoned.co.nz

Your comments on this book are welcome at
feedback@pearsoned.co.nz

Pearson Education New Zealand
a division of Pearson New Zealand Ltd
67 Apollo Drive, Rosedale, North Shore 0632, New Zealand

Associated companies throughout the world

© Pearson Education New Zealand 2008
First published 2008

ISBN: 978-1-86970-644-9

Produced by Pearson Education New Zealand
Commissioning Editor: Lucy Armour
Editor: Jan Chilwell
Page Layout and Design: Sarah Healey
Cover Photograph: Edward Gay, cliff at Oneriri

Printed in China by Nordica

Author Note

My mates and I spent a lot of time bush-walking as teenagers. We were forever getting ourselves "temporarily misplaced". We spent nights on the bare ground, caught and ate lots of fish and the occasional snake and in turn got eaten by leeches and mosquitoes. The best thing about being lost was finding our way home again. Eventually.

Scot Gardner

Chapter One

I was angry. No, I was *fuming*. I'd lost my cool a long time ago and somebody was going to have to pay.

Mr Pearson would be first. He was the closest and most responsible for this mess. He was the one who phoned Mum and convinced her that the camp would be perfect for me. He didn't *ask* me if I was interested, he *told* me I was coming. I happened to be the person standing closest when he realised he didn't have the numbers he needed to make the camp work.

"Kingy," he said, all buddy-buddy, with his hand on my shoulder for the first time in my life. "You're the man! You're the man we need next week."

"No," I said. I didn't even know what I was refusing at that stage but, if he was sucking up to me, it couldn't be good. The way he was kind of looking through me with his tanned and stubbly face, it was as if he'd chosen me for an errand and there wasn't any room for negotiation. It suddenly dawned on me what he'd volunteered me for: the wilderness camp on the Wanoom Peninsula. "I've got stuff on next week."

Vitally important stuff. Like sweeping that desiccated fly carcass off my window sill. That had been bugging me for months. Oh, and my biannual sock hunt down the side of my bed. Couldn't miss that. And what about my toenails? How was I going to find time to clip them if I was on a camp in the wilderness?

"Fantastic, Kingy. I knew I could rely on you," Mr Pearson said.

"I said no."

"I'll ring your mum and finalise the details."

"I said no."

"You'll need a backpack. School's got a spare if you haven't got one."

The next one to pay would be my mother. She'd pay for saying yes without asking me. She'd pay for not making an excuse on my behalf, like we haven't got the money to pay for the camp; like we have no camping equipment; like I'm allergic to certain tropical fruits. Never know when you're going to be hit by a rogue rambutan and come out in a rash that

makes you look like you've come off your bike onto the gravel at sixty kilometres an hour. Totally nude.

And the final head to roll would be . . . ouch! Slap! That March fly biting my arm. I really did knock its head off. It fell from my sleeve with a satisfying little death buzz and landed on the sand. I wished Pearson or somebody had warned me that those March flies like T-shirt blue.

Who ever imagined that March flies would be a pest in March? The new girl – Emily – offered me the use of her repellent and I sprayed myself until my skin was wet, but the March flies seemed to like it, too. They hung around me as I walked and descended to eat me alive whenever we stopped.

At the last packs-on stop before lunch, where we found the stinking remains of a dead animal, I checked Mrs Kennedy's GPS, which said we'd walked eleven kilometres from the car park. I guessed we had five kilometres to go and I wasn't sure if I'd make it. The straps from the school backpack had cut the blood supply to my hands and given me pins and needles for the last hour. My legs were so tired and shaky that I'd actually started praying that there wasn't too much more downhill before the campsite.

Uphill was fine. I could lean into the slope and

the pack seemed to help me grip. Going downhill, my knees felt like they were going to give way. With a tonne of camping gear on my back, I knew that, if I went down, I wouldn't be getting up again without the aid of a small crane.

The sun was hot and high. I wasn't the only one sweating little rivers. The track was a firebreak – wide enough for a car and rough enough to keep us stumbling with our heads down. I don't think there were twelve quieter school kids on the planet. Fifteen-year-olds are never quiet, except if you ask them a question in a classroom. Walking boots clomped, backpacks rubbed and rattled and we puffed.

The only other sound above the birdsong from the dense scrub and the droning of the March flies was Jye Sullivan's incessant and tuneless whistling. It wasn't particularly loud, but it had the quality of fingernails on a chalkboard. I wished somebody would tell him to shut up.

It wasn't going to be me. I could barely contain my rage without having to interact with that pus-brain. I knew from painful experience that, if I took off my cloak of invisibility by telling him to shut up, he would whistle harder and louder and every sentence that came from his mouth for the rest of

the trip would contain a curse or a put-down or a slur especially for me. He's that kind of guy.

Chapter Two

One thing I learned on that trek to Whalers Cove was that girls smell better than boys. Well, some do. My position in the long line of walkers changed a few times during the day and included a stint behind Pearson, who smelled like football socks – a whole room full of old football socks, all sweaty and cheesy. I hoped we'd find another dead animal on the side of the track to freshen things up.

Mrs Kennedy smelled like shampoo, and I walked behind her until she looked at me strangely. I felt like a stalker (well, I *was* stalking actually – moderately fragrant air, not my teacher) so I stopped to fix my shoelace and let some others pass. Emily smelled like insect repellent, which wasn't all that bad. Bethany and Rachael walked in a toxic cloud of perfume. I saw Rachael spraying herself three times.

I knew she was in pain. We all did. She'd made

it *painfully* clear that the blisters on her feet were extremely *painful*. She'd had her boots off at lunch and the blisters were quite impressive – the size of a ten-cent piece on the back of each heel and still bulging with liquid. She was in pain but, when I stumbled, she still managed to laugh at Kingy.

Most people my age would.

It's not as if I *try* to be a freak, it's just turned out that way. When I got hooked on sport, it wasn't football. I got hooked on badminton. When I got hooked on books, it wasn't skate magazines or Harry Potter, it was the old cartoons translated from French about Asterix the Gaul. When it came time to choose an instrument, I wasn't attracted to the saxophone or drums or electric guitar. I chose the tuba.

Well, to be honest, the tuba chose me. I picked it up and held it to my lips and made a sound the first time I tried. The note reverberated through my whole body and left me with tingly skin from the power of it. And a head-spin from the lack of air.

Add it all up – badminton, *Asterix*, tuba – tuck it inside a long body as lean as a skinned rabbit and you have the sort of guy nobody can take seriously. I have a little bit of common ground with everybody – even Jye Sullivan congratulated me last year when

I made it to the state badminton finals for the under-eighteens – but there's not *enough* common ground there with any one person to want to hang out.

I'm not sad about that. I'm not lonely. I've got heaps of acquaintances. Every time I go down the street in Pentland I run into someone I know. At last band practice I realised six of the seventeen members go to my school. They're mostly older than me, except for the piccolo player, who's in the same year as my sister.

She's really cute. I don't want to go out with her or anything – she just looks like a piccolo player should. Like she's got little wings tucked under her band uniform. I'm a bit too much of an elongated rabbit to look like a *real* tuba player, but the older guys who know me from band nod hello when we pass in the corridor at school. "Hey, Tuba, how you doing?"

It all seemed like it was a dream from another lifetime that afternoon. Our last pack-on stop was at a turning circle where the firebreak ended. The track from there to the campsite was only wide enough for a single person, and even then our packs sometimes snagged on the bushes. At times the canopy met over our heads, like we were walking through a tunnel. The mood of the group changed when we entered that forest. The leaf litter softened our footfalls and Sully stopped whistling. Hallelujah.

"You wouldn't want to get off the track here," Mrs Kennedy whispered.

Pearson tutted. "People get lost here all the time. Some of them don't get found. It's as if the forest has just swallowed them whole. Hungry country, all right."

"Yeah," Mrs Kennedy said. "I remember the story about that little girl last summer."

"Down at Moonrise Creek. I was here then," Pearson said. "We were staying in the campground. I helped with the search."

"Really?"

Pearson adjusted his pack. "Really truly. You don't realise how big the peninsula is until you're trying to find something the size of an eight-year-old. And the bush is thick down at Moonrise Creek, but not as thick as here. This is amazing."

I overheard their conversation and I began wondering about the likelihood of getting lost. You'd have to do something pretty stupid to lose the track. It was narrow, but it was clear enough. At times, the sides of the track were walls of matted ferns with wire-like stems. You wouldn't have been able to get off the track even if you'd wanted to.

Other times, you couldn't see a square centimetre of green among the grey trunks of tea tree. They grew quite close and straight, their stems like prison bars reaching up six metres to a thick, tangled canopy.

"Imagine what it would have been like cutting this track," Mrs Kennedy said. "I don't know how they didn't just go round in circles."

"Shh," Pearson said. He stopped and held up his hand. The stragglers eventually caught up and we stood there looking at the big outdoor education teacher.

He touched his ear and suddenly I could hear it – the one thing I'd been longing to hear since we left the cars that morning. The ocean.

Chapter Three

Without the tempting rumble of the beach in the middle distance and Pearson's persistent nagging, I wouldn't have made it. I would have settled myself down on the track and rolled out my sleeping bag on the rough ground. I wouldn't have bothered with the tent.

And I wouldn't have been alone, either. Maggie Halloran fell over with a clang and rattle. I saw her go. She hit the ground face first and hard. When the teachers helped her to her feet, she was crying and had a blood nose. Maggie would have stayed with me, but they dusted her off, mopped her down and set her walking again.

Rachael's blisters had popped and she was limping like she was barefoot on broken glass. She would have stayed, too, but Pearson had his hand on her pack, encouraging her with half a smile on his face. What is it with outdoor education teachers and their fascination with students' pain? Is it part of the entry requirements to do the course at university? Do you have to be a sadist to begin with or does that come during your study?

I would have stopped on that track, but I'm not good at admitting defeat. Never have been. The last time I cracked a spaz at my little sister Matty was when she beat me at backgammon. It was *my* game. She'd never beaten me before or even come dangerously close and I flipped out, tipped the board and all the pieces over her and stormed out. I haven't played a game since, with Matty or anybody. So maybe it wasn't the lure of the sea or Pearson's nagging that kept me going. Maybe it was just that I'm a sore loser.

Whatever the motivation was, I switched onto autopilot and concentrated on one step at a time until I heard the people ahead of me cheering. The track through the forest exploded onto the broad white beach of Whalers Cove and I knew I was in heaven. I hadn't noticed myself dying, but the vision was suddenly divine. The unblemished sand gently sloped to the azure pool that was the bay. It looked as if I could swim across to the other side – maybe a hundred and fifty metres or so – and through the mouth into the ocean beyond.

Smooth grey granite guarded the entrance to the cove, leaving a gap that would have been tight for a big old whaling ship. It was the little gap that made the bay seem so protected. The roar we'd heard came from outside the heads. The waves in the bay just hissed and licked kindly at the sand.

"What does the sign say?" Mrs Kennedy asked.

It was a piece of laminated paper stapled to a post at the place where the bush ended and the beach began.

Tina was the closest and she read quietly for a minute before scanning the beach. "Says there are the remains of a dead whale on the beach. Says we have to keep away from it."

"Where? I can't see no whale," Jye Sullivan said.

"I reckon that's it there," Mrs Kennedy said.

She pointed to a grey-black lump as big as a bus perhaps five hundred metres along the beach. It looked like rocks at first glance, but then the curves and the decaying symmetry became clear. I could see what looked like a fin.

"I don't know about you lot," Pearson said. "But I'm going in."

Packs were dumped unceremoniously and clothing shed without grace to reveal a rainbow of different swimming costumes and more skin than you'd expect to see at school.

Pearson was the first in. He wore the black running shorts he'd worn all day. He ran, hurdled the water in the shallows, then dived – quite gracefully, I have to admit – and freestyled out thirty metres or so. Kids poured in after him, whooping and screaming from the shock of it.

Rachael squealed and got straight out again – apparently salt water hurts on broken blisters. I imagined my skin sizzling as I hit the sea. It wasn't cold but it peeled away the layers of sweat and dust instantly. It left me sighing as I floated on my back, eyes shut against the afternoon sun.

Someone splashed me and I opened my eyes to see Pearson swimming for the rocks on the other side. I struck out after him, sprinting until I eventually caught up with him. Then I matched him lazy stroke for lazy stroke until we'd made it to the rocks. I found a rock I could stand on and puffed until my heart rate dropped below a thousand or whatever it was.

"Ouch!" Pearson howled. He lifted his knee out of the water. Blood oozed from a little scratch and mixed with the sea.

"Something bite you?" I asked.

The Lost King

"Yes!" he said, and I felt my throat tighten. I scanned the water we were standing in, but saw no sleek grey fish shape or pointy fin.

"Sharp oyster shell on the rock," he said.

I sighed and swam back to shore.

We came alive after our swim, found our voices and argued playfully as we set up tents in the camping area. Before we left, it had been decided by a higher power (namely Mrs Kennedy) that I'd be sharing the tent I carried with Dave Taylor, which wasn't ideal, but a whole lot better than it could have been. Could have been Michael Veener, with his scaly skin and creepy red eyes. Could have been Sully.

I didn't even want to think about that. I get along okay with Taylor. He's as tall as I am, but built more like a four-wheel drive than a sports car. He doesn't say much and that can be a good thing and a bad thing, but he knew how to set up the tent. The wind had sprung up and I limited my involvement to stopping the thing from flying away as Dave inserted poles and pushed pegs into the sand. He let me pick which side to sleep on when he was done. It felt a bit weird, but I tossed my sleeping mat in and it landed on the left, so I chose the left.

Pearson gathered us together when we were finished. It was about three o'clock by then and in my head I was ready to go home from school, but the outdoor education teacher was just getting started.

"Right you lot. Mrs Kennedy and I have sorted out your activity groups randomly. There'll be no swapping or changing. You stay with the group you're allocated and you work together as a team at whatever task you're given. Understand?"

The reply from the group was a collective moan.

"There'll be three groups of four. Starting with group one: Tina, Rachael, Dave Taylor and Dave Thompson."

Groan.

"Group two: Emily, Sully, Bethany and Kingy."

My head was ringing. I didn't hear a thing for a full minute. If I could have hand-picked my own group, it would have been *exactly* the opposite of that. Emily had let me use her insect repellent and that was the total exchange we'd had since she'd arrived at Pentland. Bethany was such a princess that it was hard just listening to her talk sometimes. And Sully . . . Why Sully? Why me?

Bethany was the first to put into words what I was feeling.

"Mr Pearson, sir, there's been a mistake," she said, sneering at Sully. "I've been put in the wrong group."

"*You're* in the wrong group?" Sully said.

They both had their arms crossed and I remembered they'd been an item last year. It had all ended rather spectacularly in the middle of an English class. There was screaming and swearing at the top of their lungs, then Bethany had stormed out crying and slammed the door behind her. She never came back into our class. She shifted into Mr Dunlop's room. That was all ancient history for everybody except those two. Ancient history for Pearson, too, it seemed.

"Don't want to hear about it, Beth," Pearson said. There was a certainty to his voice and the dismissive flick of his hand that sent Bethany storming off to the tents.

Sully was laughing under his breath.

"Group two. Where are you? Ah, Kingy, you guys have to see Mrs Kennedy. You're doing the navigation exercise first up. She's got all the gear and she can explain it to you."

Emily appeared at my elbow carrying a small plastic water bottle. "You're Kingy, right?"

"Yep."

"I'm with you, yes?"

"Correct."

"And who else?"

I pointed to Sully. She nodded. "Our other member is having a little sulk," I whispered.

She raised her eyebrows. "I see."

"We need to find Mrs Kennedy."

Emily pointed to the nest of tents. I could see Mrs Kennedy's head above the ferns. She was ranting outside Bethany's tent.

"You're acting like a two-year-old, Bethany. Get out of there now. You're not being asked to marry him. You're being asked to co-operate with him for the duration of the exercise. If you don't think you're capable of that, I suggest you start packing up your tent, because you'll be walking back out again tonight and going home."

They were strong words. Mrs Kennedy obviously knew Bethany well enough to hit her with a final offer like that. She knew it was a fairly safe bet that Bethany wouldn't be up for walking out, and she was right. A zip shrieked and a red-faced Bethany appeared beside the teacher.

Mrs Kennedy collected some gear from her pack and we met on the path at the edge of the camping area. Sully had followed Emily and me at a safe distance and now rested against a tree, kicking it

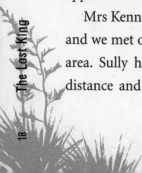

rhythmically with the back of his heel.

"Right. It's an easy and fun exercise," Mrs Kennedy began. "Here's your sheet of instructions, map, GPS and compass. There are four markers to be found. One each. They're made of yellow-painted metal and each has a symbol on it. You need to mark the place with the GPS and write the symbols here."

Sully snatched the GPS. Mrs Kennedy handed me the map and Emily the laminated sheet of instructions. Bethany got the compass.

"Share your information around. Follow the instructions. Stay on the tracks. You don't need to leave the track to find the markers. Should take you about an hour."

"What's the first instruction?" Sully asked.

"Find the sign to the car park," Emily read.

Bethany slapped the green-painted wood beside her: "Car park 16.8km".

"This is your starting location. Use the GPS to mark your starting location," Emily read.

"How do I do that?" Sully asked.

"Here, let me," Bethany said, and tried to grab the GPS.

Sully whipped it clear of her grasp. "I'll work it out, thank you very much."

Mrs Kennedy rolled her eyes, then patted my

arm and smiled. "I'll leave you to it."

Emily was looking up at me with a pained expression. "This is going to be fun," she whispered.

I could only agree.

Chapter Four

It took Sully five minutes to work out how to mark the starting point on the GPS. I spent the time checking out the map. The breeze made it flap annoyingly in my hands until Emily came and held the corner. She found the cove before I did.

The Wanoom Peninsula was roughly diamond-shaped and Whalers Cove was a bite out of the long eastern edge.

Emily followed an orange line with her finger from east to west. "Is this the track we came in on?"

"I'd say so," I said. "Or it may have been this one. Or this one. Or this one."

Emily laughed to herself. "I'm glad *you've* got the map."

"I'll swap you if you like," I said. "If it makes you feel better."

"Um, no thanks. It looks good on you. Besides,

I'm better at giving out instructions."

"Right," Sully finally said. "Starting point is marked. Next instruction."

Emily's eyes lit up. "That's me! Um ... instruction number two. Follow the track in a westerly direction for approximately one kilometre."

"One K?" Bethany whined. "That's halfway to the car park!"

"I'd say closer to six percent," Sully said, and began walking and whistling.

"What?" Bethany said.

"One kilometre is about six percent of the way back to the car park, not half."

Bethany shook her head. "Well, excuse me, Your Nerdship. Six percent."

"We're looking for a track off to the north," Emily added. She started walking after Sully.

I folded the map and followed her.

Bethany didn't move. She was rooted to the track, her arms crossed.

"Come on, Bethany," I said. "We can do this. You heard the man. A measly six percent!"

She still didn't move.

"I've got chocolate," I said.

"I don't take bribes."

"Pity. My chocolate's very special. Made from

organic sheep's intestines and everything."

She laughed. "You are a sick little puppy, Peter King. Has anybody told you that?"

I shrugged. "My mum. My dad. My nanna. A few police officers."

She was walking towards me now, hand outstretched.

I patted my pockets. "Oh, it's um . . . in my tent."

"Riiight. Get going!"

I jumped and jogged along the track past Emily. Around the next bend, I found Sully, staring at the screen on the GPS.

"Problem?" I asked.

"No," he said. He pointed to a track. It branched off to the north.

"We haven't been walking for one kilometre. Have we?"

"I don't know. Do I look like an odometer?"

"What does the GPS say?"

"It says, 'Weak signal. Find clear sky.'"

Emily had caught up with us by then. "Do you want the next instruction?"

"Is this the track?" Sully asked.

"Well, it could be," Emily said. "I don't think we've walked a kilometre though. What does the GPS . . ."

Sully huffed. "Why don't you look at the map, Queeny?"

Kingy . . . Queeny. Ha! I get it, Sully. You're being funny. Did you get it, Emily? Isn't Sully clever? I thought all that, but I didn't say it. I unfolded the map. Bethany arrived as we were trying to agree on our location.

"I think we're at this track here," offered Emily, pointing at a light orange line. It was one of three that branched off to the north. "Which means we need to go on a little further. Maybe this one. Or even this one."

"You're a natural at reading maps, aren't you, Emily?" I said.

She laughed, which is what I'd hoped might happen, but Bethany bristled.

"Leave her alone, Kingy," she spat. "At least she's having a go."

Her anger stung, but it passed quickly. We all knew this was already pushing her to her limits.

Sully wrestled with the map to find the scale, then used the edge of the GPS to measure how far we'd walked.

"I think it's the next track. This one is about five hundred metres from the start. The next one is a kilometre on the dot."

"Right," I said. "Onward?"

Sully strode off and I hurried behind him. He walked like an Olympian and I had to jog a bit to keep up. After a while, I let him go and dropped back to my own pace. The wind whipping at the canopy over my head hissed and rattled so much that I didn't hear Emily approach. She suddenly appeared at my elbow and it startled me.

"Sorry," she said and smiled. "You want some water?"

She offered her bottle. My mind jammed with thoughts. *She's offering me water. She's already drunk from that bottle. Girl germs! But, if I say no, she'll think I'm afraid of germs or, worse, afraid of her. If I say yes, should I wipe the lid before I drink? But, if I wipe the lid, she'll know I'm frightened of germs. But why shouldn't I be? I hardly know the girl! Yes, but she hardly knows you and she's offered you her only water. You don't want to seem ungrateful.*

In the end, I took the bottle, had a sip, wiped the top and handed it back to her. "Ahhh. Thanks."

"Any time," she said. "What is it with those two? Are they brother and sister or something?"

I laughed. "What makes you think that?"

"Just they way they hate each other. They hate each other the way people who secretly love each other hate each other."

I glanced at her, frowning. "Well, that makes sense. Not."

"Do you have any brothers or sisters?"

"Yes, a younger sister. Year seven."

"Do you love her?"

"Well, I wouldn't go so far as to say I *love* her. Not out loud, anyway."

"That's it! You'd never say it out loud, but I bet you *do* love her."

I thought about Matty. From this distance, I could only remember the nice things about her – when she fixes my hair or lets me have the remote when we're watching TV. Sometimes, when she gets herself a bowl of ice cream, she gets one for me without asking. For the briefest moment, my legs felt leaden and I wished I was home.

"Maybe," I said. "That's a bit heavy. I think it's simpler for Bethany and Sully."

"Oh?"

"Well, they *were* an item last year. They've been through that phase."

"I see."

"They've got to that point where they really do hate each other. I think it's genuine."

She chuckled. She had pixie dimples. She could

have been a piccolo player.

"What about you? Do you have siblings to pretend to hate?"

"Brothers. One older and one younger. Ben, my younger brother, and I have always been friends, but Luke and I have a nice hate thing going."

It was my turn to snigger.

She clenched her fists and spoke through gritted teeth. "He's just so arrogant and self-centred. He wouldn't do anything for anyone. And he's so lazy. And he's a pig."

"Yep, that's love all right."

She shook her head. "Genuine hate, I'd say."

It was easy talking and walking with Emily. She said her family had moved house so her dad could be closer to work. He was a cop – a sergeant – and he'd been transferred to Pentland from a town called Grantville, which was in the country somewhere. I think the things that made talking easy were that she was smart, she had an excellent sense of humour (by that I mean she laughed at all my jokes and offered a few choice ones of her own) and she seemed genuinely interested in what I had to say. What more could you want from a fellow activity group member?

The exact opposite of Emily – Sully the sullen

– was standing in the middle of the track with his arms crossed. "Where have you guys been? Give me the instructions, new girl."

Emily was about to hand over the card, but I stopped her.

"Swap you for the GPS," I said.

"Likely," Sully grumbled, and snatched the card. He read to himself then marched off up a new track – the track to the north.

"Right, see you then, Sully," I called. "We'll just wait here for Bethany then, shall we?"

He waved over his shoulder then vanished up the track.

"Great," I said.

"Don't worry about it," said Emily. "I can remember the next couple of instructions. We follow the track to an intersection, then we need the compass to find the first marker. He can't go far."

Emily sat. She sort of crossed her legs and lowered herself to the ground without using her hands.

"That was impressive," I said. "Do you do ballet?"

She shook her head. "I used to do gymnastics."

I sat beside her. "In Grantville?"

"Before that."

"You moved before Grantville?"

"Yeah, heaps. I've lived in nine different houses

in seven different towns."

That was hard to fathom. I still lived in the house where I pooped my first nappy. I felt sad for her then – it would be hard growing up like that.

"I like moving. Most of the time. I like making new friends, but I hate leaving them behind when we shift. I'm good at writing letters though."

"Letters? What are they? Haven't you heard of email?"

"Email? What's that?"

"That's where you get a computer and you type in your . . ."

She was smiling again. I pushed on her knee.

She shrugged. "I don't know. Email is different somehow. A hand-written letter just seems more personal. You have to make the effort to find all the bits and pieces, like an envelope and a stamp and a postbox and some pretty paper and smelly coloured pens. It says, 'I love you and I miss you' before you even start writing."

"You sound like my nanna."

"Gee, thanks."

"No, I mean, she writes . . . with a pen and a piece of paper like in the olden days. Does anybody ever write back?"

"I have three friends who I still get letters from

every time I write. Tandilka, Marnie and Sally. All from my primary school days. All from different primary schools."

"That's three more friends from primary school than I've got and I only went to the one school."

"Are you serious? Didn't any of them come to Pentland?"

"All of them did," I said. I nodded up the track. I nodded back towards the camp. I nodded at Bethany who was strolling towards us. "Wouldn't exactly call them friends."

Emily nodded thoughtfully.

"What?" Bethany said as she arrived.

"Just telling Emily that we were at primary school together."

"Were we? Where's Sully?"

Emily pointed up the track. "He went on ahead. He can't go far. He needs the compass."

Bethany offered a little self-satisfied smile and kept walking up the new track.

"See what I mean," I whispered as I got to my feet.

"Hmmm, yes," Emily said. "It could be love."

I laughed out loud at that one.

Chapter Five

"Just give me the compass," Sully growled.

"No, you give me the instructions," Bethany said.

"It's not going to happen, Beth."

"Don't call me Beth."

"Sorry, Beth. Don't you like me calling you Beth, Beth?"

"Children," I intervened. "We have to do this together. Come on, Sully, what's the instruction?"

"I've got a better idea," Sully said. "How about she gives me the compass and I save us three hours of stuffing around."

"Bethany needs to stand on that rock," Emily said. "I remember that much – the rock in the clearing."

Bethany scrambled up to the top of the rock. She balanced there and took the compass from her pocket. "Now what?"

We looked at Sully.

He swore and threw the card of instructions on the ground before storming down the track the way we came. "This is stupid. I'm out of here."

"*This* isn't stupid, Jye," Bethany howled. "*You* are."

Sully stopped.

"You're like a little primary school kid," Bethany taunted. "Go on, have your tantrum."

Sully dug a rock from the ground. "Why don't you shut your mouth!" he screamed and threw the rock at Bethany.

She squealed and teetered, but the flying rock missed her by a metre.

Sully was laughing. It was a sinister chuckle, but it made the whole scene seem ridiculous.

Bethany laughed then, too, and all the tension in the clearing disappeared, leaving only a haze of confusion around Emily and me. Seemed like it had all been a show for our benefit.

Emily looked at me as if they were mad. I could only shake my head, retrieve the instruction card and hand it to Emily.

"Two hundred and seventeen," Sully shouted.

"What?" Bethany said.

"Two hundred and seventeen degrees. Dial it up on the compass, Beth . . . *any*. Do you know how to do that?"

Emily read from the card. "From on top of the largest rock in the clearing, take a bearing of two hundred and seventeen degrees. The first marker is concealed on the tree on the edge of the clearing at precisely that bearing."

Bethany set the bearing and positioned herself. She pointed to a tree. "There!"

"I've checked that tree," Sully said.

Emily and I checked it again anyway. It took a minute to find the tag. It had been nailed into the trunk on top of a branch. Looked like Pearson's handiwork. Mrs Kennedy would have been too short for that job.

"It has a circle and the number seventy-six."

"Where?" Sully said, so I showed him.

"Glad you were here, Kingy," Bethany said. "None of us would have been tall enough to see that."

"I would have found it," Sully said. "Eventually."

The instructions told us to record the graphic and the number for later use then sent us further up the track.

"It's working again," Sully said. "There must have been enough sky above the clearing for the GPS to find a satellite. We've done one point seven six kilometres. Average speed, three kilometres per hour. Altitude, one hundred and twelve metres. Hey, it's got a compass! Ha! Don't need you any more, Beth . . . *any*."

He was whistling his irritating whistle again. I preferred it when he was Sully the sullen.

The second marker had a triangle on it and was much easier to find. It was nailed to the back of a green timber sign that said we were on the track to Mount Vereker, though the mountain itself was twelve kilometres away and, with luck, not part of our exercise. The sign had names carved in it and an empty plastic shopping bag looped over one of its posts.

We were instructed to continue still further north and had to use the number from the first marker — seventy-six — to work out which of three tracks we had to take. Bethany put the bearing into the compass again and confidently sent us off up the middle path in search of a hollow log.

The forest changed in the space of a few hundred metres. It went from small tea trees that met over the top of the trail to large furry-barked gums that flapped and swayed in the wind, dropping twigs and spinning leaves at us. For some reason or another, I felt more exposed in the taller forest. A tree rubbing against another made a moan that sounded almost human. I could feel the wind on my skin.

The track snaked and climbed gently for another kilometre until we found the hollow log. You couldn't miss it really. An old monster gum had fallen across the track some years before and a slab had been cut from the section across the track. The part of the trunk that remained was hollow and big enough for Sully to climb through at a crouch.

"Found it," he said. "Square. And the word 'right'."

"Right," Bethany repeated.

"Right," Emily echoed.

"Riiiiiight!" I sang. "One more to go."

It was the fourth marker that nearly cost us our lives. We'd continued up the side of Mount Vereker as instructed, and used our secret word ("right") to decide which track to take, when we were presented with a fork in the path, as the instructions said we would be.

I think the secret word was a little redundant though, because the intersection also had some major signage that said going left would take us to the top of Mount Vereker (ten kilometres) and right would take us to Whalers Cove (three kilometres).

Emily cheered, Bethany moaned, Sully walked and I followed.

The track ran down the hillside, switching back on itself every hundred metres or so. It felt like we were walking five times as far as if we had just plunged straight down the hill. Cutting the corner was ultimately Emily's suggestion.

"I don't know about you guys, but I can see the track just down there and I think my legs will love me forever if I go straight there rather than across and back sixty-seven times."

Sully didn't need any encouragement; he was off, crashing and banging through the scrub like a startled deer. Emily followed, with much less crashing and banging, and I followed her.

Bethany stayed frozen on the edge of the track. "Are you sure?"

"Come on!" Sully shouted. "I'm already at the track."

By the time she made it to the path again, Bethany was smiling. There was something cool about getting off-track.

Two corners further on, the opportunity presented itself again and, without any words, we followed Sully over the edge and through the scrub. With the ferns scraping gently at my arms,

The Lost King

36

I was transported to the forest of the Carnutes to hunt wild boar with Asterix and Obelix. Wild boar is their principal food – roasted whole on the fire and (in Obelix's case) eaten whole. Scrunch crunch munch scrunch.

At that moment, I reckoned I could eat a whole boar by myself, but I knew dinner would be that freeze-dried muck Mum had bought from the camping store. It was supposed to be teriyaki chicken, but the vacuum-sealed packet was clear on one side and it looked more like teriyaki polystyrene. Still, if you were hungry enough, you'd eat anything.

We emerged on the track and there was a moment of hesitation before Sully went one way and Bethany the other.

"We're going this way," Bethany said.

"No, we're heading downhill, remember?" Sully said.

It was a tough call. I pulled out the map, but Sully moved with so much confidence that Emily followed him. I followed Emily and then Bethany didn't have much choice about joining us.

Less than a hundred metres further on, the track narrowed and leaf litter began to obscure the sand.

"We're going the wrong way, I'm telling you," Bethany said.

Chapter 5

Sully didn't bite. He just kept walking.

We rounded a switchback and the track disappeared. Vanished. Dead end.

Bethany didn't open her mouth. She didn't have to. She had her arms crossed and her face was shouting, "TOLD YOU SO!"

Sully hung his head and walked past her back the way we had come.

Bethany strutted after him and Emily skulked along behind. She looked tired. "You coming?" she called over her shoulder at me.

"I um . . . have to answer a call of nature."

"Ah," she said, looking a bit embarrassed. "Good idea."

The breeze was still tossing down leaves and twigs from the tops of the gums. I had a pee, but I finished quicker than I should have. The only sound I could hear was the white noise of the wind in the canopy, and the only evidence of human activity was the faint track at my feet. I don't mind admitting that, with the others out of sight, the place seemed incredibly big and lonely. Truth is, it scared me.

I hurried back up the track and met Emily coming out of the bushes. She looked startled, but relieved to see me. I held her water bottle while she did up her belt. She thanked me and, in spite of our tiredness, we jogged to catch up with the other two.

"Might have seemed like we had to go downhill," Bethany was saying, "but actually we just needed to follow the lay of the land."

"Yeah, yeah," Sully said. "Whatever."

We walked in silence for another hour. The track followed the contours and the going was fairly easy. The bush had transformed again into low tea tree scrub and, as we pressed on, the scrub met over our heads, creating a tunnel that seemed to get darker with every step.

My guts were rumbling and carrying on. I guessed it was after six. If I didn't get a whole wild boar soon, I'd start feeling faint. So much for Kennedy's prediction that the whole orienteering exercise would take one hour. Maybe if you were an elite athlete. Maybe if you hadn't already walked sixteen Ks with a pack on your back.

Maybe if you'd stuck to the track.

When the path we were on came to another dead end, Bethany started crying. Not howling for the dead, just sniffing and wiping at her face. My chest was tight, hunger forgotten. This was serious.

"Now what?" I asked nobody in particular.

Sully turned and stomped off the way we came. "Simple," he shouted over the wind. "We head back to where we came down onto this track and retrace our steps."

He was whistling again, and I suddenly heard it for what it was: a nervous habit. The reason it sounded more like metal being crushed than birdsong was because Sully wasn't whistling for joy. He was whistling to keep the doubts at bay.

The rest of us were a little more open about the way we were feeling. Emily had that startled look on her face again, but she rubbed Bethany's arm. I thought Bethany was going to flick her hand away, but she took Emily's fingers and held them.

"Come on," I said. "We have to get back to the other track. It'll be dark soon."

Bethany dropped Emily's hand and squared her shoulders. It looked like a huge effort, but she started walking again. Emily limped after her.

"You okay?" I asked her.

She nodded. "Just a bit sore. Be glad when we're back at camp."

"You and me both."

The clouded sky through the trees turned pink and then grey in the time it took us to backtrack. The grey got deeper and heavier, until it became obvious

how dark and starless it would be when the sun finally went.

"Hurry up!" Sully yelled. He was on the edge, ready to plunge into the bush. All the greens and browns had been sucked off the plants by the impending night. Everything was drawn in shades of grey. The bush seemed even more hopeless than our dead-end track.

"You sure this is the right place?" Bethany asked.

"Positive," Sully replied, and disappeared under the ferns.

"How can you tell?"

"I just know, okay? Get moving."

Bethany cursed, but began following him up the slope.

"Maybe we should stay here," Emily said quietly.

"Come on, Emily. Not far now. Once we're back on the track, we'll be able to find our way to camp even if it's pitch black."

"You think? How do we do that exactly?"

"We feel our way. If we walk into bushes, then we backtrack until there aren't any bushes and press on."

"Right," she said. She stepped after Bethany, stumbled and ended up on her knees, almost invisible in the shadows.

"You okay?" I reached for her, but she pushed my hand away. She dragged herself upright and shoved through the ferns.

"Sully!" I yelled.

"What?"

"Wait up! We need to stick together."

"I'm not waiting up. You hurry up," came the reply.

Emily and I caught up with Bethany. She was whimpering, but pushing on. Each time she stumbled and fell, it took her a little longer to get up and start moving again.

I felt like we should have found the track by then. Even allowing for the fact that we were going uphill in the dark instead of downhill in the daylight, it seemed like we'd gone too far.

The ferns vanished abruptly and the dark space in front of us was so beautifully clear that Emily let out a little cheer.

"At last," Bethany said.

But the surface of the track was all wrong. It was hard and smooth, not rough and gravelly.

"Don't get your hopes up," Sully said from somewhere nearby. His voice was squeaky, almost unrecognisable as his own.

"Why?" Bethany pleaded. "What's the matter?

The Lost King

What's wrong? This is the track, isn't it? Please tell me this is the track."

"It's not the track," Sully said. "It's a rock."

"No!" Bethany shrieked. She sounded like she'd hid her face in her hands.

"We're officially lost," Sully declared.

Bethany curled into a ball and cried. I could hear Emily shushing her gently over the wind and figured she was rubbing her back like Mum would. I sat on the rock and felt the warmth of the day leaking out of it. It was warm on my backside, but I knew it wouldn't last. Soon all the heat and hope would be gone and we'd be left with cold hard rock.

Bethany cried for a long time. Longer than I'd ever cried in my life. I wanted her to be quiet, but I didn't want her to stop crying. Without that sad sound reminding me she was there, I could have been alone in that monstrous dark.

"Will you just SHUT UP!" Sully eventually screamed.

"Why don't *you* shut up?" Bethany bawled. "It's your fault we're lost, anyway. It's always your fault."

Sully swore at her, then Bethany swore back and

a shouting match erupted that sounded like two mongrel dogs trying to kill each other. I couldn't understand everything they were saying, partly because the rage was making their words come out broken and ugly and partly because I'd covered my ears. But their fury leaked through and made my guts tighten until I couldn't take it any more. I shot to my feet.

"ENOUGH!"

They were instantly quiet, as though they'd bitten their tongues.

"This is not helping! It's petty and it's stupid," I said.

"You have a better idea, Mum?" Sully asked.

"Shut up, Sully," Emily said. Her voice was quiet but fierce.

"Yes, I have, actually," I said. "How about you guys stop arguing?"

Sully snorted. "Yep, that's bound to save us. Good thinking, Queen Bee."

If I had been able to see him, I would have punched him. It was long overdue and I knew at least one of us would feel much better for it. But luckily it was dark. I clenched my fists and breathed hard and the feeling passed. A glimmer of hope took its place.

"How about we take stock? We nut out a plan and we take one step at a time until we're back."

The sound of the wind was the only comment.

"Right. We have a map that we can't read in the dark. We have a compass, yes?"

"Yes," Bethany said.

"Which we also can't read in the dark. We have a GPS, don't we, Sully?"

"Last time I looked," he said sarcastically, but I ignored it.

"Good. Anything else?"

"I have my water bottle," Emily said.

"Excellent. So we're not going to die."

Sully snorted. "Comforting."

But it was. At least to me it was. We weren't going to die. It wasn't cold. Wasn't likely to rain. I was hungry, and I was sure the other guys were, too, but we wouldn't die from starvation overnight. We had a little water to keep us going and were bound to be able to find more in the daylight. And a track. And a campsite.

"We're not going to die," I said again. "It's an inconvenience. We made a mistake. It was nobody's fault. We're all hungry, but it won't kill us to live on our humps. Some people have to do it as part of their daily lives. For us, it's just a . . ."

The rock we were on was suddenly bathed in a blue glow. It took me a second to work out what it was. Meanwhile, the hair prickled on the back of my neck. It was coming from the GPS in Sully's hands.

"Brilliant!" I said.

Sully laughed and directed the light at the ground like a feeble torch. The darkness was so big and complete that the little bit of blue light from the GPS display was like a floodlight to my eyes.

The girls were on their feet and we all crowded around Sully.

"Come on," he said. "Let's get out of here."

He walked off.

I stayed glued to the spot. "Wait, wait, wait. Where are you going?"

"Back to camp, numb nut. You coming or what?"

"Which way is it to camp?" I asked.

"We keep going up until we reach the track, then we follow the track to the cove. Simple."

"We should have found the track already," I said.

"No, it's further up the hill," Sully said.

"Think about it for a minute. How long did it take us to get downhill from the proper track to the other one that turned out to be a dead end?"

"Five minutes," Bethany suggested. "Ten at the most."

"How long did we push uphill through the bush before we made it here?"

"More than half an hour, I reckon," Emily said.

"Crap," said Sully. "It took me about five minutes."

"I think we missed the track, Sully."

He let this sink in for a moment. "Let's have a look at the map," he said.

I unfolded the map on the rock and he held the GPS a few centimetres off the page until we found Mount Vereker.

"Okay, we know we're on the east side of the mountain."

"How do we know that?" Bethany asked.

"We turned right when we were heading north," Emily said.

"Exactly."

Sully scanned the east side of the mountain. The trails were marked in orange and there were quite a few of them, but they looked like single strands of spider silk stretched across the wilderness of the peninsula. It dawned on me that I was looking at the map seriously for the first time that day. Looking at it like my life depended on it. No matter how hard I looked, I couldn't see a little arrow flashing red with the words "YOU ARE HERE" on it.

"The GPS!" I said. "Where are we?"

Sully looked at the screen. His face had the paleness of death in the blue glow. "We are precisely . . . Ahhh, now it's saying, 'Weak signal. Find clear sky.'"

"That thing is useless," Bethany snarled.

"Tell me about it," Sully said. For once, they agreed. "But it will be some use as a torch."

"I think we should stay put," Emily said. "Just until the morning. That way we'll save the battery and then at least, if we find some clear sky, we'll know which way to go."

"What, just stay here on this rock?" Sully demanded.

"We can collect ferns and make beds."

"What if it rains?" Bethany asked.

"We get wet," Emily said.

"You can stay here if you want," Sully said. "There are bound to be people out there looking for us. I plan to meet up with them."

"We should stay together, Sully," I said.

"Yeah, good. Stay together, Queeny. I'm going."

With that, he walked into the scrub. He and our only light were swallowed in three paces.

"Sully!" I shouted.

"He won't get far," Emily said.

Chapter 6

49

"What makes you say that?"

"The batteries were almost dead. I saw the little symbol flashing."

"He doesn't have to get far. Twenty metres and he won't be able to find us and we won't be able to find him."

"Yes, and he sleeps on his own and we find him again in the morning."

"Over here!" came Sully's voice. It sounded hollow, as if he was shouting in the school gym. Hollow but excited.

"What is it? Have you found the track?" Bethany asked.

"Come and check it out!"

Emily took my hand. Her fingers were cool.

"Hold my water bottle, Bethany," she said. "You lead, Peter."

I liked the way she said my name. Nobody under the age of forty called me Peter. It sounded proper, as if she thought I was important. I tightened my grip and began toeing my way up the hill.

"Keep talking, Sully," I yelled. "Where are you?"

Emily was right: he had made it about twenty metres. Twenty metres from our flat rock, the mountain leapt skyward as a smooth cliff face. He couldn't have gone any further if he'd wanted to.

The thing that had excited him excited the girls and me, too. A huge lump of granite had broken away from the cliff face and made a lean-to, the floor of which was clean, dry earth peppered with little animal tracks. It stretched beyond the reach of the feeble GPS light and was easily big enough to shelter us all.

Emily dropped my hand to clap.

"Oh . . . my . . . god," Bethany said. "Sully found a cave."

"Go in!" Emily ordered.

Sully handed her the GPS. "I found it. You can check it out. You know, find the best sleeping spots and that."

I could see Emily's puzzled expression in the glow, but she ducked inside the crevice with Bethany and me hot on her heels.

The cave was six or seven metres long, with a floor that was two metres across at its widest – relatively flat but sloping up to the far end. A tumble of leaves and branches blocked the far end and it was noticeably warmer in here than outside. I laughed and it echoed.

"Good effort, Sully," I said. "Could you go and find us some food now, please?"

"Right-o. One thing at a time," he chuckled.

"Found you shelter, didn't I?"

"Yes," Bethany said. "While you were being pig-headed and abandoning us."

"Shh!" Sully hissed. "Listen! What was that?"

All I could hear was my own breath and the wind in the trees.

We were all straining to hear whatever it was we were listening for, and then we heard it: a strangled "Cooee!" from somewhere out there.

There was a flurry of activity as we shoved our way outside and away from the rocks. Sully was already screaming. "Over here! Cooee! Yes! Here! Over here!"

The girls and I joined in the chorus and we yelled and whistled – well, Emily whistled: it was long and ear-piercingly loud.

"Shush! Listen," Sully said.

In the wind-rattled silence that followed, we heard another cooee. It sounded like the person who was calling had been doing so for a number of hours and their voice box was nearly shot.

We all screamed at once, with the cave acting like a sort of amplifier behind us.

"Stop! Stop!" Bethany interrupted. "Let's do it together. Cooees at ten-second intervals. Save our voices. Ready? Cooee!"

". . . eight, nine, ten. Go! Cooee!"

We continued like that for a good five minutes.

Bethany was the one who stopped us. "Okay, drinks everybody. Half-time. Anyone got any orange pieces?"

"Orange pieces?" Emily asked.

"Half-time at the footy," Sully explained. "Players get a drink and a slice of orange."

"No oranges," Emily said. "Here's the water."

The bottle made the rounds and was almost empty by the time it made it back to Emily's cool hand.

We were about to start up our choir again when we heard another cooee, only this time it nearly made me sick. Suddenly it wasn't human any more, and I realised we'd been tricked. The mangled cooee we'd heard was one tree rubbing against another, I told them dully.

"No," said Sully under his breath. "There's someone out there. I heard them. I honestly did."

As if to tease him and laugh at his puny humanness, the trees creaked again – a nearly perfect cooee.

In the horrible few seconds following that realisation, the GPS light died. Sully snatched it back from Emily, but the screen was as black as the rest of the world and wouldn't be coming on again, no matter how hard Sully shook the thing and swore. It was as if that entire scene from the cartoon of our lives had been inked in. No moon, stars or thought bubbles. Blind. Dark as death.

I bumped Emily and she took hold of my shirt. I could feel her cold fingers through the thin material.

"What do we do now?" she asked. Her voice was raspy.

The only answer was a gust rattling the tops of the trees.

"Come on," I said. "Grab hold. We'll head back to the cave."

I felt my way over the rocks. "Step up here . . . That plant is prickly . . . Just a few more metres." I could hear the sound of my voice change as we got to the gap between the rocks.

It wasn't much shelter, but it felt like home compared to the wild black forest and I wondered how the tuba would sound played inside. Pity I hadn't brought it with me. Pity I hadn't brought my dad's massive rechargeable torch and my duvet and my pillows and my collection of *Asterix* books and the lava lamp Matty gave me for Christmas. Not that there'd be anywhere to plug it in but there's something magical and soothing about the way it lumps and bubbles. I needed some magic. I needed some soothing.

I went as deep into the cave as my long legs would let me and sat with my back against the smoother of the rock walls. As I slid onto my bottom, Emily was dragged down, too, and we found ourselves sitting closer than ever in the dirt.

"We all in?" I asked.

"Yes," Emily said.

"I am," Bethany said. "Sully's still outside."

"Come in, Sully. There's plenty of room," I said.

He mumbled something I didn't hear properly, but it made Bethany scoff.

"That's good!" she snarled. "Not enough room in here for you and your massive ego anyway."

"What did he say?" Emily asked.

"Forget it," Bethany said. "Forget him. He's such an . . . arghhh! I can't stand him!"

In the quiet that followed, I think we all realised how tired we were. I heard Emily sigh. Her fingers were still attached to my shirt and I rubbed them gently.

"You're freezing."

"I know," she said. "Wish I'd put my jacket on."

"Me, too," Bethany said. "Wish I'd grabbed my sleeping bag."

"Tent would have been a good idea," Emily said.

"My sister gave me this fantastic lava lamp for Christmas. I wish I'd brought that."

The girls laughed. "You're an idiot, Kingy," Bethany said. "Has anyone ever told you that?"

"Only you," I said.

"You're an idiot, Kingy," Emily said.

It was my turn to laugh. "Thank you both very much."

"How do you stay so happy?" Bethany asked.

"Me?" I said. "What do you mean?"

"Well, you never flip out like the little baby outside and you always seem to be smiling. What have you got to smile about? Do you have a girlfriend?"

My face suddenly grew hot. I was glad it was dark. I chuckled. "Me? Ah, no."

"What about you, Emily? Boyfriend?"

Emily pulled her hand away. "No. Not at the moment. I did have. We broke up when I shifted."

"What was his name?"

"Are we playing twenty questions?" Emily said.

"If you like," Bethany said. "Would I know him?"

"I doubt it. He lives in Grantville. Jared Sinclair."

"Oh . . . my . . . god. Jared Sinclair? Are you *serious*?"

"Um . . . Do you *know* him?"

"No, don't know him. Joke!"

Emily's cold fingers made it onto my arm again. I closed my hand over the top and squeezed.

She squeezed back. Suddenly it didn't matter that we were lost. It didn't matter that we were going to spend the night in a cave. Hunger was forgotten and I didn't care that the drinking water was almost gone. I only cared about the hand on my arm.

"Imagine the colour of Mrs Kennedy's face. Ha!" Bethany said. "She's probably still wandering around out there looking for us. Yelling at the wind. She's going to be in so much trouble when my mum finds out that she made us do this stupid exercise."

"It's not her fault," Emily said.

Took the words out of my mouth. *We* decided to skip the track. *We* ignored the instructions. It seemed so innocent at the time – just a little shortcut that turned into a monster ride into the guts of this hungry country.

"Whose fault is it then? Teachers are supposed to care. They're supposed to think of everything. They're paid to look after us."

"We went off the track," Emily said. "You can't expect the teachers to hold our hands the whole time. We're supposed to be responsible. We're supposed . . ."

"*Sully* went off the track," Bethany snarled.

"And *we* followed," I said. "Emily is right. We stuffed up. And tomorrow, when it's light, we'll make it back to camp on our own."

Bethany sighed. "Wish there were some hot guys here. No offence, Kingy, but you're not my type and Sully . . . I shiver just thinking about how stupid I was going out with him."

"What happened between you two?" I asked.

"Nothing," Bethany snapped. "Don't ever go there again, Kingy. You hear me? Don't ever mention him like that again."

"Okay, okay. Sorry. Never again. Promise."

"So, Kingy, what do you actually *do*?" Bethany asked.

"Pardon?"

"What do you do? To fill in time and stuff? You know, do you hang out at Stocklands with your friends? Are you a skater boy? Bikes? Computers? What?"

I pondered the question for a minute. Normally, it was an invitation to make a smart comment, to make up a version of me that sounded like a cartoon superhero and keep the real me hidden from the likes of Bethany. But Bethany wasn't the only audience and those fingers on my arm were the truest things I'd ever felt.

"Where do I start? I play the tuba in the Pentland City band. I play badminton at state level and I love those cartoons by Goscinny and Uderzo about Asterix the Gaul and his friend Obelix. And I listen to jazz. I like jazz."

"Right," Bethany said. "I did not understand one word of that. Wait, I know badminton is a racquet sport, but I knew you were good at that anyway because I saw you in the paper last year. Tuba is a sort of drum, isn't it?"

Emily laughed, but not unkindly. "It's a brass instrument. The biggest and deepest of the brass section."

"I knew that," Bethany said. "I was just testing. So you play trumpet and shuttlecock. I know what jazz is, but I just don't get it."

"Jazz is the mother of all music," Emily said. "Jazz is making it up as you go along. It's free-form. It's . . ."

"It sounds like cats fighting to me," Bethany interrupted. "And aren't you a bit old for cartoons?"

"If you stop enjoying cartoons, then you *are* too old," Emily said.

"What's that supposed to mean? You sound like a fortune cookie."

"Just because it's animated, doesn't mean it's for little kids."

"I know that," said Bethany scornfully. "My dad watches *The Simpsons* and *Futurama* and *South Park*. He gets more of the jokes than I do."

"Little kids get *Asterix*," I said. "There are lots of fight scenes and magic potions. There are lots of puns and silly slants on history for the bigger kids."

"Sounds riveting," said Bethany, yawning loudly.

"Well, why don't you tell us some of the things *you* like, Bethany?"

"I don't have to tell you anything. You already know. You're like an old man. You like old man things. I like the exact opposite. Hot young babe things, that's what I like."

"Let me guess," Emily said. "Bands like The Long Fire, Cashmere Divas, Crownslip."

"Oh yeah! Now you're talking."

"You like bling and fashion mags like *Doleto* and *Pulse*."

"Right on."

"You shop at Scene and The Basement most of the time, but when you're cashed up after your birthday you go to Rhodes."

"Oh . . . my . . . god. You *are* a fortune cookie! How did you do that? Can you do my horoscope?"

Emily chuckled. I couldn't tell if Bethany was being serious or just playing along. Over the years, I'd realised that Bethany had made sarcasm an art form. She could pretend she was your friend so convincingly that you'd find yourself liking her and saying hi when you passed in the corridor but, if you ever tried to lean on that friendship – say, by asking to borrow a pencil or for some gum as she was handing it around – you very quickly realised it was made of tissue paper. And how she loved to watch you looking like a fool.

We were quiet for a while, though the wind in the trees kept up a constant soundtrack of creaks and groans and snapping twigs.

"We should play a game," Bethany suggested.

Emily and I didn't respond.

"Or not."

Somewhere in the distance, a tree came down. I heard it cracking through branches and felt the thud through the seat of my pants. Bethany swore. Emily squeezed my arm and snuggled closer. I patted her fingers reassuringly, but it was all a bit of an act by then. The cold and the dark and the hunger had come home to roost in my guts. I hoped she couldn't feel my pulse. I couldn't be the big brave man if she knew I was as scared as she was.

Chapter Seven

I realised that I don't need a soft mattress or a pillow or a warm duvet and a teddy bear to sleep; all I need is enough tiredness. If my body was tired enough, I could sleep on a bed of nails. That night it wasn't nails but cold rock and dusty earth, with insects buzzing at my ears and crawling on my arms.

I'd slumped to the side at one stage and I woke with Emily's head resting on my hand. The wind had stopped and the noise of the sky falling on our heads had been replaced with an even more disturbing silence. Not only was I blind, I was deaf now, too. My fingers were numb and I gently wrestled my hand free. Emily stirred.

"Sorry," she whispered.

"It's okay. My hand just went to sleep."

She sat up and I was annoyed that I'd disturbed her. I backed against the rock. "There's room here," I whispered. "You can have my arm as a pillow."

She didn't hesitate. She crawled in beside me, facing the other rock, and laid her cool cheek on my forearm. In the cold dark of our little cave, Emily could have been my sister waking from a nightmare and coming to my room for comfort. Her body warmed and we slept.

When I woke again, Emily had gone. An hour may have passed, or it could have been six, but it was still as black and cold as the inside of the fridge.

"Emily?" I whispered.

"Just here," came the reply.

"You okay?"

"Yes," she said. "Go back to sleep. We're fine."

We're fine? I curled tighter into a ball and heard sobbing. I was concerned for a second, then I realised it wasn't Emily sobbing. It was Sully. She was whispering, he was crying quietly and I was glad it was her helping him. If it had been me, I would have show him the sort of compassion he'd shown me all our lives – I'd be shouting at him, calling him names and telling him to shut his mouth, some of us are trying to sleep.

The next time I woke, the sobbing had stopped and the world outside the mouth of the cave was watery grey. The dawn was coming. We'd made it. I could barely make out the form of Bethany curled against the rock. I stepped over her and almost landed on Emily and Sully, curled together like a couple of croissants just inside the entrance. I stared at them for a long time, hoping that my eyes were playing tricks on me, but it was definitely Emily's arm around Sullivan's waist.

I had to get out. I had to stretch my body and shake the cold of the night from my limbs. Emily and me had just been about survival, that was all. I mean, I hardly knew her. We'd got close so that we could both stay warm. Like she had with Sully. The fact that he was the most arrogant, conceited, abusive and thoughtless creature on the planet didn't come into it. It was survival.

There was enough light for me to see the shadows of tree trunks around me, but not enough light to read the map. I looked at the rock face towering above and felt sick in the guts. It looked like a prison wall. There was no way we were going that way, even though it seemed like the logical place to find the track.

The birds were stirring and chattering quietly. I hadn't been up that early for years, and never in the bush. I felt like an animal – not in a bad way, but in a way that felt like the day was unfolding to me like it was supposed to. No roof and curtains to keep out the growing light, no alarm clock screaming, telling me it was time to take a shower and get ready for school.

I stepped off into the bush a short way and had a pee. I was wearing every stitch of clothing I had. I could smell my armpits, but there was nothing I could do about that and who would care anyway? When the other guys got up, they'd smell the same. For that day at least, our goals were simple – find water, maybe find something to eat and find our way back to camp.

It started raining. It was a prickly mist on my skin to begin with and I turned my face into it. It ticked on the leaves and the drops gradually got bigger until I closed my eyes and opened my mouth. If it kept up, one of our goals – finding water – would be a whole lot easier. As the canopy began to hiss, I had to turn my face from the full force of it. Finding water would be easy; finding camp might be just that little bit harder.

I turned back towards the shelter of the cave and

was startled by a hand on my arm.

"Morning," Emily said.

"Oh, hi. Didn't see you there."

"You're wet."

"It's raining."

"So it is. That's just perfect, isn't it?"

"Perfect?"

"I was being sarcastic."

"I see."

"Thanks for last night . . . letting me use your arm as a pillow."

"It was nothing."

"Keeping me warm."

"Yes, well, you did the same for me. Thank *you*."

There was a loud, theatrical yawn. "Man, I could go a burger," Sully said.

"Someone tell me we're back at camp," Bethany said. Her voice echoed from the depths. "Tell me we're back at camp and it was all a bad dream."

"No such luck, I'm afraid," I said. "Can't be far away though."

They stood around in the shelter, yawning, stretching, cursing their aching bodies and still the rain came down. Emily jiggled at the entrance for a full minute before she stepped out into it and discreetly into the bushes.

"What was all that about last night?" Bethany asked.

"All what?" I said.

"All the crying and carrying on."

"Wasn't me," I said.

"Wasn't me," Sully said.

"Crap, Sully," Bethany said. "I know it was you."

"Must have been dreaming," he said, and stepped out into the rain to find a tree.

Bethany huffed. Then she walked off into the rain, too.

They were well and truly soaked by the time they made it back to the cave. Bethany shook her hair like a dog and we all copped a spray. I unfolded the map on the rock near the entrance. There was enough light to read the features. Emily stooped close and found Whalers Cove.

"Well, at least we know where we want to be," Bethany said.

"Yeah, but where are we now?" Sully asked.

Light green on the map represented forest, but most of the map was light green. The tracks were orange. It looked like someone had spilled half a can of spaghetti on the paper.

"We need to look for tight contours," Sully said.

"Yes, tight contours," I echoed. I didn't have a

clue what he meant, but I wasn't about to ask.

Emily looked at my face, but I stared at the map.

"What are tight contours exactly?" she said eventually.

"See these little black lines – they're contours. They measure height above sea level and tight contours mean steep country."

"Steep country like our rock face here," she said.

"Exactly. Give me the compass," Sully said and held out his hand. Bethany looked at it but didn't move.

"Compass!"

"I'm not so sure that's a good idea. The GPS was in your gentle, caring hands, too, remember?"

"Fine," Sully said. He ripped the map from the rock and trudged off into the rain.

"Sully!" I shouted.

"Get back here, now!" Bethany ordered.

Emily jogged after him, but he didn't stop.

Bethany squealed through gritted teeth and followed.

I patted the rock where the map had been, thanked the cave for the shelter it had provided and started walking.

Chapter
Eight

The rain wet my hair through to my skull and found its way down my collar. It made me shiver, but I wasn't really cold. Moving through the bush was keeping me warm. I could see steam rising faintly from Emily's shoulders.

Nothing more than a few curses were muttered for the first hour of walking. We followed Sully blindly through tall ferns and sparse forest, over rocks and ever downhill. I had no idea where we were. I had no sense of which way we needed to go. If following Sully was all we needed to do to keep our group together, then I could do that. If we stayed together and kept moving, sooner or later we'd find . . .

A track. Sully stood in the middle of the path with his fists on his hips and a self-satisfied smirk on his face. He didn't have to say a word – our sense of relief at finding a trail was like a badge he could wear, but it didn't last long.

Bethany pointed one way.

Sully shook his head and pointed the opposite.

"Let's look at the map, shall we?" I suggested.

Sully unfolded it on the gravel. The paper had become wet and fragile. Bethany laid the compass on the top and I rotated it and the map so that they both pointed north. That much I did know.

"So we're looking for tight contours?" Emily asked.

Sully nodded. "Tight contours on a hill falling away to the east. A hill that has a track running across it."

"What about here?" Emily asked. Her finger was shaking and I wanted to grab it, rub it and breathe on it like my mum did when I was a little kid. "Here's the rock face. Here's the eastern slope. Here's the track."

Sully was nodding. "Or here," he said. The three features were right there again under his finger, a full fold of the map away from where Emily had found them.

"We haven't travelled that far," Bethany said.

"Here then," he said and outlined the eastern slope and a track in another spot, even closer to Whalers Cove.

Three different mountains, three different tracks. I followed the orange lines back and, regardless of which one we were on, Whalers Cove was to the right – the way Bethany had suggested.

"We have to go south," I said. "The way Bethany suggested."

"You can go that way if you want," Sully said. "I know the way I'm going."

Bethany moaned. "Don't be such a pig-headed loser, Sully. It's logical."

Sully grabbed the map, spilling the compass onto the track. He folded it roughly and headed north.

"Sully! Stop!" I barked. "Talk us through it. If you're so sure we should go that way, explain it so that we know what you're doing."

He unfurled the map again and it tore along a fold.

"Careful!" Bethany screeched.

Sully shot her a look but pointed at the map. "What if we're on a part of the track that's cutting back across the slope? Like here or here or here or here. What then?"

It instantly made sense to me. "If we're on that part of the track, then heading south will take us further away from the cove."

"Exactly. We want to head south, but we want to

head *downhill* even more than that."

"I don't get it," Bethany said.

Sully shook his head and pointed the way he was going. "Downhill."

Yes, downhill, but only a little.

It was as light as it was ever going to get that day. The sky was dirty grey sink water, but the parts of it that dropped on my head and found their way into my mouth were only salty from my own sweat. Emily filled her plastic water bottle from a trickle on the side of the path. It was crystal clear and we drank a bottle each before moving on. After fifteen minutes of snaking our way downhill, Sully's track changed its mind and climbed sharply.

"I thought we were supposed to be going downhill?" Bethany asked.

Sully didn't bite, just kept walking ahead like he hadn't heard her.

We were picking our way through boulders, the track scarcely more than a line where the leaf litter was thinnest. The canopy closed over us again and the path plunged back downhill. Bethany confirmed with the compass that it was taking us north – exactly the opposite direction to the way we wanted to travel.

"I have a feeling we're going the wrong way," Emily said.

"Then I'm not alone," Bethany said.

"Sully! Wait up!" I hollered, but he'd already stopped.

He had his head cocked and his hand out like he was listening for something. Then I heard it, too.

A low, pulsing throb. A helicopter. It was off in the distance, but I doubted it was carrying tourists on a joyride.

It must be looking for us.

"We need some open ground," Sully shouted. "Come on! Run!"

Suddenly, our tired bodies weren't tired any more and we were moving like true wild animals through the undergrowth, following the faint trail, slipping and crashing.

The canopy opened like magic and a slab of marble sky rained down on us. We couldn't see the helicopter but that didn't stop us from shouting and frantically waving our arms above our heads.

"They can't hear us!" Sully shouted.

"Yeah, but someone else might," Bethany howled. "Heeeey! Over heeeere! Cooooeee!"

The chopper never came into view. It sounded as if it was coming closer, then drifted off in another direction. Got louder, teasingly, then vanished altogether.

"Don't worry," Sully said. "It'll be back."

"Now what do we do?" Emily asked. "Do we stay here and hope it finds us or do we keep moving?"

"We stay here," Sully said.

"What if it doesn't come back?" Bethany asked.

"Then we start walking again."

"It could be hours," I suggested. "Maybe they're concentrating their search somewhere else?"

"Yeah, and if it comes over while we're in the forest, there's no chance they'll see us, is there?"

"Wish I'd worn my fluoros," Emily said.

"You've got fluoros?" Bethany asked.

"Jacket. Pants. All back at camp."

"We'll wait here while you go and get them," Sully sneered.

"I was just saying," Emily said.

"Leave her alone," Bethany growled.

Sully stomped into the centre of the clearing and sat with his back to us.

"He's like a four-year-old sometimes," Bethany whispered.

"Or a two-year-old," Emily said.

"Was it him crying last night?" I asked.

Emily nodded.

"What about?"

She hesitated, then shrugged. "He didn't say."

"He's pretty messed up," Bethany whispered. "And I'm saying that in the kindest way I can."

"I think he's scared of the dark," Emily hissed.

"Are you serious?" I asked, but Bethany was already nodding.

"Scared of the dark, spiders, bees, caterpillars, needles, cockroaches, heights, losing things. You name it, he's scared of it."

I thought about that for a moment and tried to make sense of it. Fear of spiders and heights wasn't so unusual, but *caterpillars*? It was ironic that Mr Toughness could be scared of caterpillars, but in the same breath it was sad.

"Imagine what he would have been going through last night," I said. "I've never been in any darker dark than last night."

"He wouldn't come any further inside the cave," Emily said. "He was freaking out and his breathing was going weird. I didn't know what to do."

"Should have left him," said Bethany bluntly.

"The thought did cross my mind." Emily flashed me a glance. "I was quite comfortable where I was, considering the circumstances."

I smiled and huffed a laugh.

The Lost King

"Then I thought, what if it was me who was freaking out? What would I want? So I patted his hair and put my arm around him and he clung on to me like a . . . like a two-year-old."

For some reason, hearing that made me sigh. It was good that Sully had fears. It was even better that Emily had said she'd been comfortable with me.

"What's the story with you and Sully?" Emily asked Bethany.

I held my breath, but Bethany didn't explode. She pushed her wet hair off her face and shrugged. "We went out. It was ages ago. When I was young and stupid."

"It ended badly?"

Bethany snorted a laugh. "Could say that, yes."

Emily stared at her, but Bethany avoided her gaze. That was as much as she was going to say.

I shivered, my breath forming little clouds of steam.

"My legs are about to fall off," Emily said. She lowered herself into that gymnast's squat and I sat beside her. My bum was already wet, but the earth still felt cold through my clothes.

"Can I lean against you?" she asked.

"Of course," I said.

"Back to back."

We slid around and her shoulders felt warm against mine, but only for a few seconds.

"Me, too," Bethany said. "Wriggle over."

We let her in, but the tripod of bodies wasn't nearly as warm as Emily and me, back to back. I wished Bethany and Sully could kiss and make up – just until we returned to civilisation.

"I spy with my little eye . . ." Bethany began.

Emily and I moaned.

"What? We have to do something."

So we played a game. We played I Spy around and around until Emily gave us an S word and it wasn't sky or sun or snot or sick or slime. So we sat in silence and shivered for a while. Bethany could make her teeth chatter.

When we finally gave up, Emily told us the word was sand. I could hear her stomach rumbling.

"What's your favourite food?" I asked her.

"Me? Mango. That's easy. You?"

I had to think. Fried dirt would have been my favourite meal if it was in front of me right then. "My mum makes this seafood paella with mussels and scallops."

"Oh, stop it," Bethany grizzled. "That's cruel."

"What about you, Beth?" Emily asked.

"My name's Beth*any*."

"Sorry. What about you, Beth*any*."

She was quiet for almost a minute. "Fries."

"Are you serious?" Emily asked. "All the beautiful food in the whole world and you choose fries?"

I, felt Bethany shrug. "My tastes are simple and I simply have to have the best. Really good fries are the best food in the world."

I wanted to disagree but my mouth was full of saliva and I would have dribbled.

"It's stupid really," Bethany said. "I never eat breakfast so I've only really missed one meal – dinner last night – but I feel so hungry. Hungry like I'm going to die if I don't eat soon. I'm wondering which one of you guys I'm going to have to kill first."

Emily laughed.

"I'm not kidding. Miss one meal and suddenly I start thinking like a cannibal."

"If you lived in some parts of Africa, this would be your normal state of being," Emily said.

"Yes, well, we're not in Africa, are we?"

I had the urge to run some more, to get hot and turn my wet clothes into a sort of sauna. Try and dodge the hunger that was slowly driving me mad, too. I stood and the girls moaned.

"Come on," I said. "The helicopter's not coming back any time soon. We can't just sit here. There's

Chapter 8

food waiting for us back at camp."

"Mmm," Bethany said as she stood. "I've got chocolate in my pack. Provided Rachael hasn't scoffed the lot. If she has, I'll eat *her*. Yuck, on second thoughts . . ."

Emily took her time getting up. When she did, she hugged herself and jumped on the spot.

We assembled around Sully.

"We're moving out," I declared. "The chopper isn't coming back."

"Right," he said. "See you at your funerals."

"Don't be an idiot," Bethany said.

"The golden rule when you get lost is to stay put."

We all laughed at that one. Coming from Sully, that was a great joke.

"When did you remember that rule?" Bethany said. "Five minutes ago?"

"What if the camp is five hundred metres down that hill?" I suggested. "How stupid will we look?"

"Stupid and *alive*," he said. "What if it's ten Ks further, back the way we came?"

"We haven't come ten Ks," Bethany said.

"Fine, you get moving. When the helicopter picks me up, I'll tell them you're somewhere down the hill."

"The golden rule when you get lost is you stay

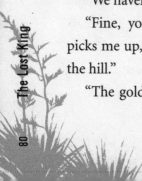

together," Emily said. "I know that much."

"True," Sully said. "You stay together down the hill and I'll stay together here."

Bethany took Emily's elbow. "Come on. We know where he is if we need to find him."

"So you're going to stay here?" I asked.

He nodded.

"Until you're found?"

He nodded again.

"Okay, we're going to follow this track. If it goes somewhere useful, we'll come back and get you. If it doesn't, we'll backtrack and get you anyway."

He dismissed us with a wave and looked at his boots.

Chapter Nine

We found a faint trail on the downhill side of the clearing. It disappeared into the scrub and I took the lead. Ten steps in, I disturbed an animal, but it crashed off before I could see what it was. Maybe it had made the track? The path was clear and obvious in some spots, as if it had carried a lot of traffic. In other spots, the doubts crept in.

"Here!" Emily said. "Look."

A twist of faded pink marker tape was tied to a branch. It was the first sign of life we'd found on any of the tracks since we'd taken the shortcut and it spurred us on. Emily spotted another piece, and then Bethany found one that didn't seem as old. What with the tape and the slope, we were practically jogging through the bush.

Over our clumsy footfalls and the tacking of the rain in the trees, I heard a sound. Not a pulsing helicopter, but a good sound, just the same – the rush and surge of the ocean.

Ten minutes later, we arrived.

It wasn't an arc of white sand but a cliff face. There were no tents assembled at the far end of a cove, but bits of battered timber and rope were poking from between craggy rocks. The cliff was sheer and there was no obvious way to get down to the water line.

Emily gripped my sleeve and peered over the edge, scanning the rocks in both directions, then looking out to sea. Suddenly, her face crumpled and she started crying. I tugged her away from the edge and held her. She buried her face into my shoulder. Bethany looked at us both, puzzled.

"Shh, it's okay," I whispered.

"I . . . thought . . . I . . . thought . . . we'd made it," she sobbed.

"We're one step closer," I said. "We're at the edge."

Bethany huffed. "Fat lot of use that is to us. We still don't know where we are."

"But we *do*," I said.

Emily let go and wiped her eyes with the back of her hand.

I unfolded the map. It tore a bit more but, with the three of us holding it, it was readable.

"We're at the edge of the map. Where the land

meets the sea. Here," I said. I ran my finger along the eastern edge of the peninsula. "No clearer track in the world. Now which way do *you* think we should go?"

Bethany cursed and took the compass from her pocket. The wall of rock stretched to the north and to the south. We were north of Whalers Cove, and not very far north. We all pointed south together.

"I think we'd better get Sully first."

We backtracked carefully, from pink ribbon to pink ribbon, stopping and starting and crossing the slope. We were following a path we'd only been down ten minutes before, but already it had been swallowed up by the sameness of the grey-barked trees and the rain. No wonder we were lost. The trail was another fragile lifeline – if we took three wrong steps, we might never find it again. I wished I had a smart little dog with a good nose like Obelix's dog, Dogmatix. He could find a wild boar or a Roman soldier in the depths of the Gaulish forest. Maybe even a camp full of school kids.

The loud crack of a branch made me take my eyes from the path. It had come from beyond the roll of the hill. At first I thought it was just another animal put to flight by our messy human bumbling,

but then I saw movement as the thing vanished – a tuft of dark fur.

Fur or hair?

"Sully?"

More cracking of branches timed to the slow rhythm of human footsteps, not scampering animals.

"Sully!"

"Kingy?" came the reply. In time, the dome of his head appeared over the edge of the hill. He jogged a few steps.

"What were you doing?" I growled. "You were supposed to be waiting in the clearing."

He shrugged, but his face was red, and not from exertion. "I just . . . I didn't hear the chopper again and I thought it'd be better for us all if we were together."

"Scared of being on your own more like," Bethany whispered.

That made more sense than Sully's story. Since when did he care about anything or anyone other than himself?

"You know how close that was?" I said.

"What?"

"If I hadn't seen your head . . . and I only *just* saw it . . . we never would have found you."

The colour drained from his face and he chuckled nervously. "No, we would have met up again."

"How? Where?" I held out my arms wide and he looked around.

"At the gates of hell?" he suggested, with a bit of his usual bravado.

"You are an absolute . . ." Bethany said, but I shushed her with my hand.

"We've found the coast. We're going to pick along the cliff edge back to Whalers Cove. The helicopter will have a better chance of seeing us and we have to come to the cove eventually."

"Excellent. Lead on."

Bethany went first and, for the first time since we started out, it felt like Sully wasn't driving the bus. It was also the first time since we'd left Whalers Cove that I actually felt like I knew where we were going. My head ached, my feet were sore and my belly had given up on being hungry, but at least we weren't travelling blind.

Chapter Ten

We arrived on the edge of the cliff at almost the same place we'd left it. Sully had a grin on his face for the first time in days.

"Man, that's spectacular," he said.

For a moment, the clouds of desperation at being lost lifted and I saw the view in a new light. It *was* spectacular. Breathtaking, in fact, but we weren't there to sightsee. We were trying to get out of there.

And then we heard the helicopter again. It was faint and it was gone five seconds after we heard it, but hope began to rise.

I unfolded the map again.

"We reckon we need to head south – that we're somewhere along the coast here," I said, and traced the edge of the peninsula again.

Sully nodded and pointed over his shoulder but didn't say a word.

The cliff we were perched on continued south-east for several hundred metres before a point obscured the view. It looked like we'd be able to travel along its edge if we were careful. The bush ended and the rock face started abruptly, as if the edge of the peninsula had been cut with a long sharp knife.

His confidence renewed, Sully pushed past Bethany and began slogging through the shoulder-high shrubs that clung to the edge of the cliff. Bethany rolled her eyes, but she followed and at last it felt like we were getting somewhere.

Emily and Bethany fell into one of those girly conversations where they just talk about anything and everything. Seemed like the only real goal of the conversation was to use up words. I only listened in on bits. Mostly I listened to the ocean and the sound of us pushing through the wet scrub, but there were bits that stuck in my head.

"Who do I miss?" Emily said.

"Yeah. At home. Who do you wish was right here with us now?"

Emily hummed for a few seconds. "My dad. If my dad was here, there'd be no way we'd be lost. He's a gun with maps and compasses and everything. We parked the car in the city one time and I realised

that, if he hadn't been there, we would never have found it again. Never. We would have lost our car. Mum and I went back to the car before him and she couldn't even find the *car park* where we'd left it. She had to phone Dad and get him to come and take us there."

"True? Mine's the exact opposite," Bethany said. "My mum has the great sense of direction. My dad is hopeless. If he's driving and Mum's not telling him which way to go, we're in a constant state of lost. It's become a joke. We call it Dad's Scenic Route."

I thought about my own parents then. They both had pretty good senses of direction. They helped each other out when they were in unfamiliar territory, but they were like that about most things. They had been old friends before they were husband and wife and they looked after each other all the time. I know that, if I'd had a rational argument for not coming on this stupid camp and I'd presented it to them both, they would have discussed it – in agonising detail – and then left the decision up to me.

Why hadn't I put up a fight? I wondered what they were doing right now. If word had got out to them that I was lost, they'd be here on the peninsula somewhere, looking under every bush. Dad would have taken time off work and Mum would have taken Matty out of school. They'd be cold and wet. Matty would be crying, but it wouldn't stop her looking for me. If I wasn't found – dead or alive – my dad would keep searching. He would look until the day he died.

My throat grew tight, my eyes blurry with tears.

I'm okay, guys. I'm coming.

It doesn't take long to work out that scrub – any scrub – looks easier to get through than it really is. It took hours to cover the couple of hundred metres to the point we had seen. There was a mad urgency to our efforts as we punched through that final patch of bush. We were rushing to see the new view on the other side of the point, but it offered no reason to smile. Just more dense bush, cropped low by the wind coming off the ocean. More sheer rock face. More broken rocks foaming in the surf below. No sand. Our new view was obscured by another point, twice as far away as the first.

I felt all the strength drain out of my tired limbs, as if someone had deflated my balloon. Emily and Bethany slumped down on a rock, their faces wrinkled poems of desperation and hopelessness. I knew *exactly* how they were feeling. We were officially lost, but we knew where we had to go to be found. Our bodies were aching, hungry, cold and clapped out, but we were strong enough to get where we needed to go.

It wasn't all *that* far. It *couldn't* be. But it was so much further than any of us wanted to go, except maybe Sully. He'd glanced down the coast, shrugged and kept walking. Walking and whistling his tuneless mess of a whistle.

Bethany waved him off with the back of her hand. Emily took a sip from her water bottle and handed it to me. I didn't wipe; I just drank. Then I handed it to Bethany, who scrubbed at the top with the hem of her wet T-shirt before taking a token swallow. We rose, like zombies from the grave, and followed Sully.

The undergrowth we dug through had a sameness about it that made the journey feel like a loop. Nightmarish thoughts crept into my aching head. What if we *were* going in circles? The drop-off was a harsh reality to our left, though, which meant we *couldn't* be going in circles. But what if we were going the wrong way? That thought hurt and I did my best to think about other things. It *had* to be the right way.

We were travelling a safe distance from the

edge of the cliff, but occasionally one of us would dislodge a rock and send it skittering over the edge. Sully picked up stones when the view to the water was clear and pitched them as far as he could. It looked like fun, but it also looked like it took up energy I couldn't afford to waste.

There was a heart-stopping moment when I heard Emily stumble and shriek. I looked up in time to see her water bottle tumbling between rocks and over the edge.

"No!" she howled.

We scrambled over the wet boulders and peered down.

The bottle wasn't cartwheeling into the sea. In fact, I couldn't see it at all.

"What did you lose?" Sully asked.

"My water bottle."

"Don't worry about it," Bethany said. "It's not like we're going to run out of water."

"It's just down there," Sully said. He was standing on the rock, right on the edge, peering down. "I can get it if you want."

I lay on my stomach and slid forward. The bottle was resting on a rock ledge, out of reach, but not too far down.

"How could you get that?" Bethany asked. "You

can't reach that!"

"Easy," Sully said. He stepped between the boulders where the bottle had fallen and crept forward.

"Don't," Bethany scolded. "It's too dangerous."

Sully kept moving. "Yes, Mum."

"Sully!"

"Grab my hand, Kingy," Sully said. I took his cold fingers and he shifted the grip so that we were holding each other's thumbs like a bikers' handshake.

"Don't worry about it," Emily said. "Let it go."

"Can't leave your rubbish behind," Sully said. He crouched and reached for the bottle.

I could feel myself being dragged over the rock. "Sully . . . I'm . . . slipping."

"Got it!" he crowed. He pulled back and his fingers went loose, but I didn't let go until he was safely back between the rocks.

Bethany was still shaking her head. "You're a total moron."

"What?"

"What if you had fallen?"

He shrugged. "Save walking."

"I thought you were scared of heights," said Emily, taking the bottle.

"Who told you that?" Sully said and stared hard

at Bethany. "I love heights."

"You're an idiot," Bethany said.

"And what does that make you?"

He bumped her – deliberately – as he made for the front of the line again. She slapped the side of his head. It must have hurt, but Sully just kept on walking.

Chapter Eleven

The rain eased some time in the early afternoon – some time after my guts had stopped nagging me that I'd missed yet another meal. The rain eased and the wind whipped up. We heard the helicopter again and again, but they were obviously looking on the other side of Mount Vereker, because we only ever heard it for a few seconds and it never flew into view.

Our next pain came in the form of a gorge. It was invisible when we were looking along the coast, but it was painfully obvious when we got to it – sheer walls of smooth rock four metres apart, dropping six metres into a working washing machine of surf. It gouged inland for a good hundred metres through bush that held too many shadows for my liking.

Sully swore. Bethany swore. Emily looked at me with that helpless poem on her face again.

"How do we get across?" she asked.

"We don't," said Sully bluntly. "We go around."

Then Emily swore, too.

"You got that right," I said.

Sully led on again, but it was hard work following the gorge inland. Hard work was the last thing our tired bodies needed. The trees were bigger, but not big enough to walk under. The uppermost branches were right in our faces; the lower ones scratched cruelly at our arms and legs. For a while, we hardly seemed to be moving forward at all.

"This is stupid," Bethany groaned. "There has to be another way."

"Just shut up, will you? Shut up!" Sully spluttered. "There is no other way. Just shut up and keep walking."

Luckily, the trees got bigger as we trekked further inland, ducking under branches that had previously slapped at our faces, crouching and crawling through the tangled limbs below. They kept on getting bigger until the canopy was well above our heads and we could walk between straight grey trunks. That easy walking lasted a total of about fifty metres before we were met by a thicket of wiry ferns like those I'd seen on the side of the track coming into Whalers Cove.

"Now what?" Bethany whispered to me.

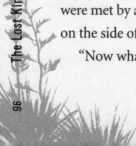

The thicket was easily three metres high, dense down to the forest floor and ran inland as far as I could see. There were rough holes in the tangle at various places along the ground – small holes that would have been perfect for animals that scurried on all fours. Perfectly useless for upright human animals.

"We go through," Sully said. He tucked his chin into his neck and walked headlong into the ferns. But he'd only gone two steps before the thicket stopped him. He backed out and dusted himself down.

"We go over," he said, and charged at the wall of greenery, jumping as high as he could. The ferns gave way and seemed to swallow him. He kept on climbing, crushing the mess underneath him as he went, until I could only see the top of his head. He paused for a breath and then he was off again, scrabbling and clutching at the wiry stems, paddling hard just to stay afloat.

In two minutes he'd travelled about three metres. I could still see his head, but he was sinking. Then he spun around and began fighting back towards the edge again. When he tripped and dropped onto his hands and knees in front of us, he was puffing like he'd run a marathon. A six-metre marathon.

"Maybe we could go around it?" Emily suggested.

"It's following a little creek," Sully said. "It could go on forever."

He paced out a small circle on his hands and knees until he came face to face with one of the animal tunnels under the jungle. Then he flattened out and crawled, commando-style, into the hole.

"We go under," he called, his voice muffled by vegetation.

"No way!" squeaked Bethany. "I'm not going under there!"

Sully had crawled out again, but his eyes were lit with enthusiasm. "Fine," he said. "You wait there. There might be a bulldozer on the other side. If there is, I'll come back and get you."

Bethany pelted him with abuse. There was steam rising off her – some of it was literal, most of it figurative. While she was fuming, Emily and I got down on all fours and followed Sully into the cool, dark, wet world concealed by the thicket. My back was barely covered before Bethany was behind me, urging me on.

For someone who was supposed to be scared of the dark and spiders and so forth, Sully seemed to be enjoying himself in that underworld. The animal tunnel twisted and turned and at one stage seemed to be hooking back the way we came. There were intersections, and a pile of bleached bones and feathers. Still Sully wormed on.

The ferns released a sort of brown powder if you got hooked on them. It hung in the air and clagged in my throat. Soon the others started coughing and spitting. I left a metre's gap between Emily and myself that got harder to maintain as we crawled deeper under the thicket and Bethany urged me on from behind. At one point, Emily stopped moving forward for a full minute. I could hear Sully burrowing on, but Emily was stuck. Forwards, backwards; there were frustrated yelps then full-on thrashing and panicked screaming and squealing.

I grabbed her leg and shouted her name. She kicked at my hand and started backing into me. She was crying and freaking right out. I rolled to the side and let her retreat until I could grab her and hug her tight. She squirmed and raged, but I hung on and kept saying her name over and over again.

Slowly, the terror began to fade. She stopped screaming, but she didn't stop puffing hot breath onto my neck. Her whole body shook uncontrollably. Behind us, I could hear Bethany sobbing.

"What was that?" Sully called back.

"Nothing," I said. "She just got a bit of a fright, that's all."

Sully swore.

"What?"

Suddenly, he was moving faster, grunting and scrambling through the tunnel.

"Sully! What is it?"

Then I heard it, too – the chopper. Loud and clear and getting louder.

At that moment, I felt cursed. If we'd been prisoners on the run, this would be the perfect place to hide as the helicopter made its pass. The ferns were so thick above us, we'd have been safe from gunfire. But we weren't on the run. We weren't trying to hide. I wanted to be on top of a granite mountain, holding six burning red flares as the chopper flew over, not in the belly of some monstrous plant beast.

Man, it was close that time. It was so close that the whining jet engine drowned out Bethany's screams of despair – she was howling from right by my feet. I could feel the rotors chopping up the dusty air, sending it into my lungs. But it came and it went without pause, as lost to us as we were to it.

When there was nothing left to hear but sobbing and the noise of the wind, I peeled Emily off me and looked at her face. Her eyes were still shining with fear, her mouth cramped and wet with saliva.

"You okay?"

She nodded feebly.

"Want me to go first? That way you can hang on to my pants or my boot or whatever and I can make the path a bit bigger."

She nodded again and wiped her mouth.

"What about you, Bethany? You right to go?"

"Just get moving. We've got to get out of here."

The trail that Sully had left was a bit like a bulldozer's. It splashed across the little creek where Emily had the sense to stop and fill up her bottle. It curled up the gentle slope on the other side of the creek and exploded into what at first seemed like a clearing, but turned out to be thick-canopied forest. Still, the light was much brighter now that we were out from under the thicket.

Sully sat on the damp earth, his arms around his raised knees and head hanging.

"That was close," I said.

He sniffed and spat. There was a trail of blood on the side of his neck.

"You okay?" I asked. "What's the blood on your neck from?"

He wiped his hand under his chin, smearing the blood trail, then leapt to his feet in horror as he saw his hand. Blood had begun to pool on the collar of his shirt.

Bethany stepped up to him. "Let me look."

To my surprise, he leaned back and exposed his throat to her.

"It's just a little spot, but it's bleeding like . . ." She squealed and jumped back.

"What?"

She lurched forward again and flicked something off Sully's collar.

"What was it?" Sully said, his voice broken and almost a scream. "What was on my neck?"

"It was one of those bloodsucky things!"

"What? A mosquito?"

"No, one of those slimy bloodsucky things."

"A leech," Emily said. Her voice was surprisingly calm.

"Yes! A leech!" Bethany said. She hopped in circles and rubbed her hands together.

Sully was wiping at his neck, his face contorted with disgust. Bethany lifted up the leg of her pants and began examining her own skin.

"Here's one," Emily said. The leech was a little black stripe just below her left knee. She raked her fingernail over its head and it dropped to the forest floor. A bead of blood instantly welled where it had been attached. She found another on her ankle, but it hadn't started sucking.

My legs seemed to be clean. I was about to declare myself leech-free when I found a tiny one inching along my finger. Revolted, I shook my hand as hard as I could, but it wouldn't come off.

Emily caught my forearm. "Stand still."

I did as I was told and she flicked the bloodsucker into the forest. Bethany was still twisting and turning, trying to inspect the back of her legs. Then she was squealing and shaking her hands and dancing.

"Stop!" Emily barked.

"Get it off me, get it off me, get it off me . . ."

Flick. Flick. Flick.

Dance. Dance. "Get it off me, get it off me, get it off me."

"Hold still!"

Emily scratched at its head with a fingernail and it was gone.

Bethany stopped dancing and sighed. "Oh, my god, thank you, thank you."

Sully had already started walking again, following the edge of the thicket back towards the coast.

"Wait up!" Bethany called.

"No!" he barked. "You *hurry* up. When that helicopter comes back, I'm going to be seen."

Chapter Twelve

The scratching branches, the grasses that tore at my clothes, the March flies – they all took a piece of me. Maybe that was what Pearson meant when he called this place "hungry country". It would eat you alive given half a chance. I'd finally make it to Whalers Cove and all that would be left would be rags holding bloodied bones together.

We heard the helicopter over the wind from time to time. It was a little injection of adrenalin, making my weary heart race and sending me scurrying for higher ground. It came and it went in a matter of seconds and we never actually saw it.

Its teasing only added to the sense of the whole misadventure being a cruel outdoor education nightmare. Maybe there wasn't a helicopter at all? Perhaps it was just Pearson with a megaphone pretending to be one. The whole thing was a set-up to see how we'd perform half-starved and clueless. At any minute, Pearson would dive out of the bushes and shout, "Okay, that'll do for today. I've seen everything I need to see. You've all failed."

But we hadn't failed. Not yet, anyway. Nobody had said anything other than a random curse since we'd made it through the ferns. We weren't moving very fast, but we were moving. We hadn't made it back to the coast, but we weren't far away and, when we got there, we knew which way to go.

We were still together. Bethany was limping a little. The blood on Sully's neck had darkened and grown a crust. Emily slipped backwards off a low branch and I caught her – as if it was a dance move and we'd planned it – but she had no spare energy for smiling. She thanked me in a whisper and kept walking. She had the determination of a robot but – like all of us – her batteries were running down.

We made it to the coast as the grey day turned even gloomier. I couldn't decide if it was the approaching blue-black storm clouds or the sun setting that masked the remaining sunlight but, whatever it was, it took the tiny shine of joy off finally making our way around the gorge. It had taken hours to get around that four-metre gap. We stopped on the edge, sipped from Emily's water bottle and I checked the map.

"Here!" I said. "We're here. Look . . ."

Bethany looked over my shoulder. Emily and Sully didn't move.

"There's the gorge. Here's Whalers Cove."

"Could be," Bethany said. "How far?"

I counted the squares on the map. Each one represented a kilometre between the camp and us. "Six . . . maybe seven Ks. That's all."

"What?" Sully cried. "How is that possible? We could not have walked as far as we have and still be seven Ks from the camp."

I shrugged, but I had my theory. The scrubby point we'd passed earlier was a little blip on an otherwise straight shoreline north of the bays. We first arrived on the coast even further north than that. We'd made a huge triangle, the long side of which rolled down Mount Vereker *away* from the camp. We'd done a lot of extra Ks just to keep going downhill. Thanks, Sully.

"We could make it," Emily said. "We could make it before dark. I can walk at nearly five kilometres an hour. I reckon we have about two hours until dark."

Sully scoffed. "It's nearly dark now."

"Well, maybe we should just sit here then, Sully," Bethany mumbled as she stood.

"There's no way you could walk five Ks an hour through this stuff," Sully moaned. "Even if there was a track."

"So we arrive after dark," Emily said. There was hope in her voice again and I could feel it tingling in my own limbs.

"Come on, Sully," I said. "It's worth a try."

"Of course it's worth a try," he said. "Just don't get your hopes up."

He began pushing through the undergrowth again, with Bethany hot on his heels.

"If my hopes aren't up," Emily mumbled, almost to herself, "then I'm just about ready to lay down and die."

It was tough going, even with a little bit of hope to chew on. We hugged the edge of the cliff and found ourselves climbing a hill. The ocean had cut a slab out of the side of a mountain and we realised halfway up its craggy slope that we'd have to turn inland again. It was just too steep.

The forest on the side of the mountain was much friendlier than on the coast, but we still had to climb. We were all shaky-limbed and I had the sudden thought that, if we had to stop there for the night, we would all freeze. There was no cave to hide in on that mountain. The heavy dark clouds looked as if they were about to burst with rain and, if they did, I knew my little core of heat would be quickly drowned. When I realised that, the last of my hope faded and in its place I found a panic that kept me moving.

"Come on, Emily," I said, as I took her hand to help her over a stump. "We have to keep going."

She rolled her eyes as if to say, "Tell me something I don't know."

I let go of her fingers, but she held on. We were still holding hands when we made it to the ridge and discovered a wide, flat plain of low grass that stretched as far as we could see. A kind of plateau.

Sully started skipping. "Now you're talking! Five Ks an hour, here we come."

Emily dropped my hand and looked at me with a tired smile. "Thanks," she whispered.

I nodded and smiled back. I wanted to tell her that I liked holding her hand, that I'd do it whenever she wanted, but I think she'd worked that out already. As much as I liked holding her hand, the fact that she didn't need me to was a good sign. It meant the terrain was easier – at least that's what I told myself as I clenched my fingers on the last of our shared warmth.

The grass was mostly knee-deep. It was soft to the touch and the wind brushed its surface so that it rippled like water. We pushed on, following animal tracks to small clearings, and eventually the surface underfoot became squishy. To begin with, it sucked at our boots and made disgusting squelching noises. Then the black soil turned to mud and a wall of tall reeds met us. The wall went off in both directions for hundreds of metres and the reeds hissed and rattled like a living thing – a fence with a word or two to say about those passing through it.

Sully didn't hear what it was whispering – or if he did he chose to ignore it and crash his way onwards. The reeds bent and cracked easily under him, the mud grabbed at his ankles, but he kept walking and we followed. Gradually, the mud grew deeper and colder. It was midway up her calves before Bethany found her voice.

"It's a swamp, Sully. Let's go back."

"Go back if you want. We're nearly there."

"How can you say that? How can you know that?"

"I just know, okay? Come on, don't stop."

She wasn't going to stop; I could see that on her face. She looked like I felt. I wasn't going to stop because that hungry land under my feet might swallow me whole. Bones and all. Without a trace.

I realised how close we were to being added to that list of people lost and never found. If the swamp went on much further, we'd never make it to the other side. We'd go until we were exhausted, realise we weren't going to make it right across and by then it would be too late – we'd be too tired to get back.

The fear really got hold of me then. It clamped around my chest until I couldn't breathe. I pulled my leg from the mud too fast, leaving my shoe behind. I stumbled and fell forward, my arms sinking instantly up to my elbows, my face far too close to the foul breath of the swamp. I panicked and started yelling and scrambling to get up, but only managed to dig myself deeper, and then my leg cramped. The muscles in the back of my thigh felt like they were being torn from the bone. My yelling turned to howls of pain and I kicked and straightened my leg, finally coming to rest face down on the mud.

Hands clawed at my shoulders on both sides and dragged me upright – Emily and Bethany, shouting my name and shaking me.

"It's okay, Peter!" Bethany screamed. "We're nearly there. You're okay. We've got you."

"Come on, Peter. We have to keep moving," Emily said.

"I've lost my shoe."

"Where?" Bethany asked. "Where is it?"

"In one of my foot holes. I . . . I got a cramp. Sorry."

Emily found my blackened shoe and we staggered on as a wonky tripod across the last of the mud. There was a gap in the reeds where Sully had bulldozed through and we followed his track to a pond where there were no reeds at all. Sully was halfway across – waist-deep and unsteady on his feet.

"It's not as bad as it looks," he said. He didn't sound very convincing. "It's just water. There's no mud."

"What about leeches?" Bethany moaned.

"Don't know, don't care," Sully said. "We'll sort that out later."

The water felt warm after the mud. Sully was right – it was much easier to move through, and our tripod made good progress.

At one point, Sully disturbed a duck and it honked and flapped and crashed through the reeds, narrowly missing Bethany and setting us all laughing. It was as though a pressure valve had popped.

We clawed through the muddy reeds and made it free of the swamp onto a bank of low grass. Sully was still laughing. "Did you hear Beth squeal when that bird flew out? That was *such* a good squeal."

"Shut up, Sully," Bethany said, but she was still smiling.

"Scared the crap out of me, too," he said. "I didn't squeal though, did I?"

Emily handed me my shoe. She'd cleaned it somehow.

"Thanks."

"You okay?"

I nodded.

"What happened?"

"I . . ." I said, and paused. I was about to tell her a story and cover up my weakness. Pretend that there had been *something* out there – something sharp, something with teeth, something with claws – but the truth fell out instead.

"I thought I was going to die. I thought we were all going to die."

It was the truth, with not even the slightest polish of lies to make it look better.

"I started freaking out. Just caught me by surprise."

There was nothing cold and hard about that truth – it was bright and warm and it brought tears to my eyes. Emily wriggled closer and put her arm around me.

"It's okay. We're going to make it. We're nearly

there. Come on, we have to keep moving."

I dragged my wet shoe over my wet sock and followed the others through the grassland back towards the edge of the world.

When I caught up with Emily, I took her hand and kissed it. "Thanks," I said.

She flashed a smile with those piccolo player's dimples and squeezed my fingers. "I owe you more than that."

The view from the south side of the mountain was the one we'd been hunting for: the bush rolling away to the rocks and, beyond that, a flash of sandy beach that seemed to glow in the fading light.

"Is that it?" Bethany shrieked. "Oh, my god, is that it? Please tell me that's Whalers Cove."

It was still a long way off, but it was most certainly the cove.

"See the big lump, halfway along the beach?" I asked.

"The whale!" Emily cooed.

"Yes!" Sully hissed.

"I can see people!" Bethany said. "Right down the end. Look."

She pointed and we followed her arm. There was

a group of tall, thin ants at the far end of the beach – almost certainly people. As we watched, a bright light flashed, sending us into a screaming, waving frenzy that lasted a full minute before we gave in to the reality that nobody could hear us over that distance. Over the wind. Over the sound of the waves at their feet. Not a chance.

"Come on," said Sully through his teeth. "Let's do this."

Chapter Thirteen

The last of the light seemed to vanish like a broken bulb as we picked over the rocks into the forest on the south side of the mountain. The hunger was back with a vengeance. My guts felt as if they were well on the way to eating me inside out and there was nothing I could do about it, except walk.

I hung close to Emily, with Bethany limping behind Sully. We were close enough that I could hear their small grunts of exertion every time we had to get up over a rock or a tree, but they kept disappearing in the dark.

"Sully!" I called. "Wait up!"

"Come on, King," he replied. "We have to keep moving."

"We're not going to make it," Emily breathed. "Not tonight."

Sully wouldn't have been able to hear her.

I knew she was right. It wasn't giving up – it was stating the facts. It was dark and getting darker. We were exhausted and that wasn't going to change any time soon. I just wanted to curl up in a ball beneath one of the ferns in this sea of green and shadow we were wading through. I wanted – no *needed* – to rest my burnt, exhausted body.

Up ahead, Sully had stopped and he and Bethany were arguing, but not like dogs – more like diplomats.

"I know what you're saying, Beth, I really do," he said. "I'm falling apart, too. But we're *so* close."

"What is it?" I asked. "What's the matter?"

"Sully found a shelter."

"Again?"

He took my hand and dragged me down to knee height. A boulder with a bite taken out of it had come to rest with the bitten part close to the ground. I could only see the shadow, but there was something about the way the sound moved around that made me think it was a small cave.

"You're amazing," I said. "How big is it?"

"I don't know. I don't want to know. We have to keep moving. We're so close. They're looking for us. They're waiting."

His breathing was all ragged and it took me a

moment to realise he was crying.

"Hey, Sully, it's okay. We're okay."

Sully stood and swore. "You might be okay, but I'm dying here. I've had enough. I want out. *Right now.*"

I heard him wrestling around in his clothes, then the forest lit up with the glow from the GPS.

"Whoah!" I said. "How did you do that? I thought the batteries . . ."

"They are dead. They just had a chance to recover. They won't last long."

He was on his knees, inspecting the gouge under the rock. There was dry, dirty sand and animal poo and the cave floor was the size of a two-man tent. It sloped sharply at the back of the space. There wouldn't be much room to roll over.

"Stay here if you want," Sully said.

"What are you going to do?" Bethany asked. "Where are you going?"

"I'm going to try to make it," he said. "I have to."

"Don't be a bonehead, Sully," Bethany said.

"We have to stick together," Emily said.

"So stick together. I'm going."

Curling up in that hollow seemed such a perfect idea. I'd had enough of Sully's pig-headed determination. It was certainly the thing that had kept us moving all through the day, under thickets and through swamps, but it was probably the major reason we were lost in the first place.

Let him do what he wants, I thought. I felt like the parent. I felt like the dad and my kid was running away from home and I knew the best thing to do was to let him go. Sully wouldn't get far. He'd run out of light and then he'd either find his way back to us or he'd bed down where the torch ran out. I hoped it didn't rain, for his sake.

"It's okay, Bethany, let him go," I said. "He has to try."

Silence.

"Here," Emily said and handed him the water.

"Thanks," he said. "I'll bring back people and torches. And food. We'll find you."

"Give me a drink before you go," Bethany said.

"Me, too," I said.

We all drank, leaving him with half a bottle.

"Right," he said. "See you soon."

"Sully?" Bethany said.

"What?"

"Don't . . . don't do anything stupid."

"Yes, Mum."

"I mean it."

There was a hole in the night, the wind stopped

raging and the forest fell silent, just for a moment.

"Thanks," he said, and he and his little blue light vanished into the ferns.

I set to work digging out the dry sand and piling it along the mouth of our little shelter. My body wouldn't stop shaking – my hands, my jaw, my shivering spine. It was easy digging, as long as I didn't rake my fingernails over the rock too often. Soon there was a hollow easily big enough for the three of us and, if we lay close enough, all four would fit.

"Hurry up," said Bethany, through chattering teeth. "I'm freezing out here."

I dragged myself most of the way clear. Bethany pushed at my arm. "I'm in the middle," she said. "You first . . . no, Emily first, then me then you."

"Whatever," I said. "Just get in."

I held my hand on Emily's head as she wriggled into position at the back of the little space. She didn't hit the rock; in fact, she had plenty of room. "There aren't any spiders in here, are there, Kingy?"

"I can't guarantee that," I muttered, my teeth clenched against the cold. "But, pretty soon, I don't think you'll care."

Bethany shoved me out of the way and made a lot of noise as she shuffled into position beside Emily. "Quick, Kingy. Get in here before I change my mind."

I backed under the rock and Bethany grabbed me with her cold hands and hugged on tight.

"Hope you don't need the toilet in the night."

"I went before," she said.

"Wwwwhen?" Emily stuttered.

"When we were in the swamp."

"You went in the pool?" I said. "That is disgusting."

"Me, too," Emily squealed, and we all laughed. Laughed and snuggled tighter.

"We should play a game," Bethany said.

Emily and I let out a perfectly timed groan.

"I know . . . I spy with my little eye something beginning with the letter B."

"Ummm," Emily said. "Is it blackness?"

"Yes! You're great at this game. Your go, Em. Can I call you Em?"

"You can call me anything you want while you're so lovely and warm."

"Why don't you like being called Beth?" I asked.

"Yeah," Emily said. "I noticed Sully gets away with it."

"Shut up," Bethany said, but she sounded like she was smiling. "I don't know. Sounds like death . . . or something. I've always hated it."

"I like Beth as a name. Death*any*," Emily said bravely.

Bethany laughed again. "I know, a song! Let's sing a lullaby. Ummm."

She started singing. It was a ballad I recognised – a Cashmere Divas song I'd heard on the radio about a thousand times. Emily was a fortune cookie after all. Bethany *did* like the Cashmere Divas. I wondered how she knew that.

Bethany's voice was sweet and soothing, even right in my ear:

"You bring light to my night,
Shade to my day.
You make me feeeeeel all right,
What more can I say?
You sweep the webs from my heart
And put the shine in my eyes
You make me feeeeeel all right,
I'm not a ghost town."

Emily made a sound like a distant roaring crowd. I clapped my hands.

"That was beautiful," Emily said.

"Thank you. Your turn."

"I can't sing," Emily said. "Not a note. Besides, I don't know any songs."

"What about you, Mr Bandgeek? Sing us a song?"

"I um . . . I . . ." I said, and then a song popped into my head. Ten seconds later, we were all singing the chorus from the Monty Python song "Always Look on the Bright Side of Life" and whistling. Emily was right: she couldn't sing, but she could yell and she whistled like a bird. We kept getting louder and louder, until I started to wonder if we might dislodge the rock we were under, killing us all. It didn't matter by then though. I would have died happy, quickly . . . and warm.

"Kingy?" called a voice from the darkness.

"Shhhhh!" I commanded. The song ended abruptly.

"Kingy?"

"Sully?"

I sat up and cracked my head on the roof, then lay back down again, moaning.

"Keep talking," he said. "Where are you?"

"Over here . . . here . . . here. Ow."

"You okay?" Bethany whispered in my ear.

"Fine," I groaned and rubbed at my forehead. "Low ceiling in this apartment."

I heard a body moving through the bushes, a

hand on the rock. Then the hand was on my knee and I took it and dragged him towards me.

"Watch your head," I said. "The rock is hard. You okay? Get in close."

He was shaking badly and I hugged him in a tackle. He backed into me and I felt like the parent again. The runaway had returned. He was crying and whimpering. Bethany reached across me and held his arm. He hugged in tighter and took her hand.

"It's okay, mate," I said. "You did your best. We'll find them in the morning. You're safe now. We all are. We're going to survive, I know we are."

Chapter
Fourteen

I'd be lying if I said I slept well, but I did sleep. The wind died sometime during the night and the mosquitoes found us. I didn't mind if they sucked my blood – they could have as much as they wanted, as long as I didn't *hear* them.

I woke a few times as somebody jiggled and blew at the darkness. My body ached and I badly wanted to roll over, but the effort would have been huge, requiring much more energy than I had at my disposal. So I slept in bites and starts. One time when I woke, Sully was crying again. He sounded so strange – alien almost. I wondered if he was crying in his sleep. I patted his arm and shushed in his ear and he eventually snuggled in and stopped sobbing.

I could smell us in the morning – all sweat and stale breath mixed with damp dog. Emily woke us all by scrambling over the top, apologising as she went. She needed to go, she said – desperately.

"Should have just wet the bed," Bethany moaned. "At least it would have been warm. Come back!"

"Ah, it would have been more than wetting the bed, I'm afraid," Emily said, and Sully rolled outside to set her free.

There was a chorus of moans as we stretched and bent the life back into our cold limbs. Then Sully broke wind, loudly.

"Charming," Bethany said.

"What?"

I let one rip, too, and Sully chuckled.

"Disgusting!"

We had breakfast when Emily returned – the last of the contents of her water bottle – and soon we were walking again, in the shadows before dawn. I'd hate to think what time it was. Totally uncivilised animal-human o'clock, that's for sure.

Sully led the way, as usual, but he was looking over his shoulder, making sure we were close by. Nobody mentioned last night's unsuccessful attempt to find help, but we did talk about food.

"Burgers," Bethany said. "One with everything and I'd just keep eating them until I spewed."

"That's feral," Emily whispered.

"I wouldn't eat burgers," Sully said. "Not first,

anyway. I need something to get the rotten taste out of my mouth and a burger wouldn't do it. I'd have mango. Mango or pineapple. A whole mango and a whole pineapple."

"Melted cheese on toast," Emily said. "And a big bowl of tomato soup."

"Yesss," I agreed.

"For breakfast?" Bethany whined. "You think *I'm* feral."

"Roast boar," I said. "Three of them. Whole."

"Stop it," Sully said. "You're making me dribble."

He changed direction suddenly and we stopped in our tracks. We'd been picking our way down the rocky hill and he'd spotted something more beautiful than the idea of three whole roast boars – a track. And it was heading in the right direction.

Bethany couldn't contain her excitement and she hugged him around the neck and jumped up and down. He hugged her back, then made a token effort to push her away, but he was still smiling.

"I can't believe how easily I've survived without food," Bethany said. "I reckon I got hungrier doing that forty-hour famine."

"Did you do that?" Emily said, sceptical. "Raise money for hungry kids by not eating?"

"Of course . . . and I didn't cheat."

"You amaze me sometimes," Emily sighed.

"Hey, I'm *full* of surprises."

It *was* slightly amazing that Bethany had done something as big as going forty hours without food to help the lives of others less fortunate. But *full* of surprises was a bit of an exaggeration. I wondered if maybe it was Emily who was *pretending* to be surprised.

"That's about how long we've been missing," Sully said.

"Seriously?" Bethany squeaked. "Only forty hours?"

Sully snorted. "We're not back yet. We can go another forty if you want."

Bethany tucked in her chin and ran past Sully up the track. Sully bolted to catch her.

Emily smiled. It wasn't a beaming grin with piccolo player dimples. It was a tired smile that looked as sad as it did happy.

"Do you think she really went without food to help someone else?" I asked.

Emily shook her head. "I think she probably did it, but not so that someone else could eat. Did it because her friends were doing it. Did it with the dumb thought in her head that going without food for forty hours would change her into a slimmer, more attractive Bethany."

"Ah, I see," I said. "How is it that you know so much about her without her having to tell you?"

She shrugged. "I've made a lifelong study of her species."

I scoffed. "That's a bit cruel," I said, though I'd have to admit to being a tiny bit guilty myself.

"It's true. For a long, long time I wanted to be someone like Bethany. I thought that was what I needed to do to be liked. You wouldn't *believe* how hard I've tried. Never really worked though."

"What? Are you saying that you can't be a superficial cow with attitude even when you *try*?"

She laughed. "That's pretty cruel, too."

"Cruel, but true. Well, a little bit true."

"I gave up trying. I made a pact with myself when we moved to Pentland. I decided that I was only ever going to be the real me. They could like it or lump it."

I sucked air through my teeth. "Scary stuff. How are you holding out?"

"Well, you be the judge. You're my first serious experiment."

"Me?"

"Yep. It started when we were sitting on the track waiting for Bethany. Do you remember that?"

"The day before yesterday?"

She nodded and hung her head in guilt.

"Oh, I remember that. That's the real you? The gymnast with the nine different houses in seven different towns?"

Her mouth hung open. "You remembered!"

I nodded. "If that's the real you, I want a year's subscription."

She blushed then. And that set me off; I had to up the pace to hide my own embarrassment.

"Don't go so fast!" Emily groaned, grabbing at my hand. "I'm already dying." She pulled at me until I had to stop. "Can you give me a piggyback?"

Up ahead, Bethany and Sully had stopped in the middle of the path and turned to look at each other.

Bethany's eyes lit up. "Helicopter!"

"High ground!" Sully shouted.

"The rocks!" Emily screeched.

She jumped at the side of a huge boulder but couldn't find a handhold. I grabbed her leg and hoisted her as high as I could reach while her toes scrabbled at the surface. Then she was off up its steep slope until she disappeared from sight. I lifted Bethany the same way, but she didn't have the gymnast's touch. She collapsed back onto me and we fell to the ground, laughing.

The drumming was getting louder and we tore around looking for another rock. The one that Bethany chose to climb didn't make it clear of the trees, but it got much closer than the trail. She was shouting and screaming and waving her arms over her head. Emily was squealing, too, and further along the track. Sully's voice box sounded like it was about to shred with the exertion.

I ran back to Emily's rock and made an almighty leap for the handhold. The rock was slippery under my boots and I had to haul myself up with my arms. When my shoes finally found purchase, the helicopter sounded like it was right overhead, though I couldn't see it. I clawed and slipped up the face of the boulder to a place where I could see a slab of the grey sky, but the helicopter had passed by then. We'd missed it and it had missed us.

"Don't worry!" Sully yelled. "It'll be back."

Emily was nowhere to be seen. The rock fell away steeply in every direction and I was on my own at its peak.

"Emily?" I called. There was no answer.

And then I saw it. Twenty metres downhill, a patch of blue amid the leaf litter – Emily's empty water bottle.

"Emily? Emily!"

"What is it?" Bethany squealed. "What happened? Oh, my god, no!"

From her rock, Bethany could see something and she was hysterical. She jumped clear and ran.

I swore as I ground my fingernails down to nothing sliding back the way I'd climbed. When I ran around the other side of the rock, I found Bethany staring up, with her hand over her mouth and tears thick in her eyes.

Emily was hanging upside down, wedged between two rocks. Her arms hung over her head and I couldn't see her face. She wasn't moving.

Chapter Fifteen

"Get her down!" Bethany squealed. "Get her down. Now! Hurry."

There was blood on the rock beneath her and I could only just reach her fingers.

"Emily! Emily, please. Take my hand."

Then Sully was beside me, swearing and making little panicked whimpers. "Lift me up!" he said. "Quickly! Lift me and I'll be able to reach her."

I held his foot and he crawled up the face of the downhill part of the rock. He could reach her shoulders and he tried to lift her, then swing her and pull her free. "Emily!"

Nothing worked. He lost balance and I caught him on his way down.

"She'll have to go *up*," Sully panted. "We have to lift her. Lift me again." He moved into position and I shoved him up the rock.

"Let me stand on your shoulders," he cried.

He held the rock and I put his foot onto my collarbone. The tread of his shoe bit into my skin as he shifted his weight and his other foot swung into place on my other shoulder. Now he could hold himself steady between the rocks. I scuffed and slid until I was directly underneath her.

"Hold my legs," Sully said. "Balance me."

I did as I was told and he grew suddenly heavy. I could feel him losing balance. I couldn't hold him. I stumbled clear of the rocks and Sully came down on top of me.

Emily came down on top of him. She was moving. Her eyes flashed open, her pupils like two dark caves, then she screamed and grabbed her leg, howling and writhing and struggling for breath. She ripped at the soil and kicked. Blood exploded from her nose and showered me as I grabbed her, trying to stop her from smashing into the rocks in her agony. I cradled her head and she bit my shirt.

The helicopter made another low pass. Bethany and Sully jumped and screamed until the bird had gone again. They were both coughing and spitting at the dirt.

Emily rocked and moaned and swore in whispers. She had hold of my arm and I knew her nails were making me bleed – tiny drops compared to the flood from her mouth and nose.

"Find some water," I yelled. "The bottle is down the hill. Hurry."

I wiped tears from her face and looked in her eyes. They were alive with pain. "Where does it hurt?"

"My ankle, my ankle, my ankle."

"Bethany, here. Get her shoe off."

"No!" Emily barked. "No, no, no. Leave it on, leave it on."

"Can you stand?"

She shook her head.

"Come on. We have to try."

I put her arm over my shoulder and hauled her to her feet. She wasn't heavy, but she wailed in my ear so loud it hurt.

Sully returned with half a bottle of muddy water. "Sorry, that's all I could find."

"It's fine," I said. I helped Emily to a low rock and sat her down. She was still swearing under her breath. I kept hold of her hand.

"Oh, my god," Bethany said. "Are you all right?"

"What sort of a stupid question is that?" Sully said. "Look at her face, for god's sake."

A blood nose and a small cut on her bottom lip had given her a red moustache and beard that was dripping onto her shirt. I took off my own shirt and wet it with the brown water. I wiped her chin but she pulled away.

"Sorry," I said.

She took the shirt and soaked up the blood herself, then spat some out on the ground between her feet.

"It's not as bad as it looks," she said.

"What happened?" Bethany asked.

"I slipped."

"Obviously," Sully said. "What happened to your face?"

"I think I must have hit the rock face-first."

Bethany held her own mouth.

"Anything broken?" I asked.

She tentatively felt her nose, then shook her head. "Only my ankle."

"That's stuffed up our five kilometres an hour," Sully said.

"I can carry you," I said.

"We'll take it in turns," Bethany said. "Piggyback."

"Put your shirt on, Kingy," said Sully, trying for a joke. "You're giving me snow blindness."

I helped Emily clean up the blood she'd missed and dragged my wet and bloodied shirt back over my head. She blew her nose in her hand and wiped it on the dirt before beckoning for help up.

"Eww," Bethany screeched. "I'm not touching that. You just blew your nose on it!"

I crouched in front of Emily and she hung on around my neck.

"Gently does it," I said, and stood.

She was light, as far as piggyback passengers go. I thought I could carry her all the way if I needed to. All the way back to Whalers Cove and the waiting helicopter. All the way back to Pentland.

It took her a few wriggles to get comfortable, but when she did I felt her warm cheek against my back.

"Thank you. You're an amazing person."

I chuckled. "I think that blow to the head has done you some damage."

"No," she said. "I'm serious. You're amazing."

"That's enough," I said. "One more flattering lie and you'll have to hop back to camp."

"You *are* amazing. *And* you can't take a compliment. Why is that?"

I thought about making a smart comment, but my heart wasn't in it. I was wasted. I felt closer to Emily than I had to anybody outside my family. I sighed.

"Do you need a rest?" she said.

"No, that was a sigh of relief."

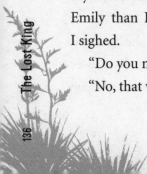

"Oh?"

"I can't take a compliment because it's easier and much safer to treat every nice thing anyone says as sarcasm. You know, 'Gee your hair looks nice,' when what they're really saying is, 'Man, hold still, there's a dead animal on your head!'"

Emily struggled to swallow a laugh. "I didn't say anything about your hair and, if you want my honest opinion . . ."

"No! I know it's bad, but you know what I mean?"

"Of course. This is a beautiful time of our lives and we're all so loving and generous."

"Exactly! Sometimes I hate being a kid. Can't wait for it to be over. I hate being stuck in that shark tank they call a school. I hate having adults patronise me because I live in a kid's body."

"I don't think you're alone there, Peter."

"Peter? Who's Peter?"

"Sorry. What do you want me to call you? Kingy sounds so . . . I don't know . . . punch-in-the-arm-barbecue-sporty."

"So make up a name if you like."

"Could I call you Pete?"

"Not very inventive. If you must."

"Right, I'll call you Pete and you'll call me Em. Or Emmy."

"Or an-Emily?"

"What's that supposed to mean?"

"Anomaly. Get it? Sorry, bad pun."

"Ha ha. What does anomaly mean?"

"You know, something that's not normal."

She slapped my shoulder. "Thanks very much."

"It was supposed to be a compliment."

"Sounded like sarcasm to me."

"I like Em. I like Emmy, too. You know . . . please make welcome the Emmy-award-winning Emmy Hale! Huzzah! Huzzah!"

Her cheek was warm on my back again and I felt completely alive. Dead tired, aching to the very core of my being, but oh so alive.

"We're going to make it, aren't we, Pete?"

"Even if I have to carry you all the way."

Chapter Sixteen

Sully and Bethany kept up a vicious pace. We were near the end and we all knew it. I could feel Emily alert and urging me on without saying anything. She was the jockey and I knew what I had to do – just get us there, right to the end of the track, as fast as my scratched and bruised body would take me. Into the arms of the ant-people we saw yesterday, so that the whole experience could become a memory, instead of this cold and insect-bitten reality.

When we rounded a sharp corner in the track, Sully and Bethany were waiting for us.

Sully stepped up. "My turn to carry the cripple."

"Thanks very much," Emily said.

I thought we'd given up on the sarcasm?

"I'm fine," I puffed.

"Don't be a hero, Kingy," Bethany said. "It doesn't suit you."

"What's that supposed to mean?" Emily asked.

"It means we share the load," Sully said, slapping his own back.

"No, it means Kingy is much better at being a dorky nerd than a hero."

I felt Emily stiffen. "What, like you're better at being heartless and shallow than a reasonable human being?"

Bethany's jaw dropped like she'd been slapped.

Sully sucked air through his teeth. "Ouch! Felt that one."

"Shut up," Bethany growled.

"No, *you* shut up. Pete just carried me . . ."

"Oh!" Bethany interrupted. "It's 'Pete' now, is it?"

Emily just kept on talking. ". . . more than a K on his back. In my view, that makes him a hero."

"Yep," Sully said. "I think you're a hero, too, Kingy. Now it's my turn. Let's go."

I gently lowered the fiery Emily to the ground. She took her own weight slowly, swearing under her breath at the pain.

Sully slipped into position and hoisted her aboard. He bucked her up and she settled into position, biting her lip.

"Okay?" he asked over his shoulder.

"Fine," she said, through gritted teeth.

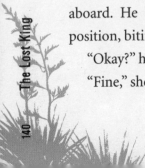

Bethany waited until they'd moved some way down the track before she mumbled, "Once a dork, always a dork. That's what I say. You two were *made* for each other."

I grabbed her shoulder and spun her around. She shrieked and her hands came up to defend herself.

I let her go. I was a full head taller than her and I used every centimetre of it to show my rage. "Enough!" I snarled.

I left her there, frozen to the track, and jogged to catch up with the others. I didn't look back. I didn't care if she stayed there for the rest of the day – I'd said all I needed to say to her.

"I think she's a bit tired," Sully said.

"That's no excuse," Emily said. "We're all tired."

"I think she was at the end of her rope before we even started this stupid trip," he said. "Maybe she's always at the end of her rope."

I remembered her singing the night before. It was a dumb song, but somehow it had made the darkness seem friendlier. "She's doing okay."

Sully couldn't see Emily grinning at me. "We're all doing okay. We're going to make it."

Half an hour plodded past. Bethany crept up on us and I got a fright when I saw her.

She smiled. "Sorry."

Emily strained to look at her over her shoulder.

"Sorry," Bethany said again. "My turn yet?"

Sully swung around – a full one-eighty that made Emily grab on tight.

"Yep," Sully said. "Your turn . . . if it's okay with the jockey."

"Of course," Emily said. "I'm only worried for Bethany's back. Sure you'll be okay?"

"See how we go," she said.

Emily mounted up and Bethany's first three steps were a bit wobbly, but she wriggled and jiggled until her load was balanced and charged off up the track.

Can't afford to judge people, I thought. No sooner have you put them in a box than they hop straight back out again. Everybody. The Sully I knew and loved to hate two days before was gone. In his place was a smart, determined, fragile kid with more than his fair share of guts.

And I'd never be able to look at Bethany the same way again. Maybe we'd get back to school and she'd be just like she was before, but I'd heard her sing away the darkness. She'd helped drag me out of the scariest place I'd ever been and we'd kept each other warm like we were brother and sister. That sort of thing changes people. And Emily. Oh, Emily . . .

We all heard the helicopter at the same time.

We ran – even Bethany with Emily on her back – to a spot on the track where the tops of the trees opened and the sky was clearly visible. It was flying low.

"Wait for it," Sully screamed. "It's coming. Wait for it."

We were dancing on the spot in anticipation and the chopper got louder and louder. I wished I'd gone to the toilet. I could imagine the embarrassment of being hauled into the cabin of the whirlybird and their having to leave the doors open to get rid of the smell of pee.

So what?

It was too low. It seemed to be flying below us. The rotors thundered and the jet engine whined. I realised it had stopped moving. The jet started winding down.

"It's landing!" I yelled. "It's landing on the beach."

Sully sprinted.

"Wait here," I said to Bethany.

"No way!" she squealed.

"Leave me here," Emily said. "Come back for me."

"No way!" she squealed again. She grabbed Emily's legs tighter and ran.

I opened my stride. Gave it everything I had left. I ran as though my life depended on it, because at that point it felt like it did. I bolted along the snaky downhill path, the air tearing in and out of my lungs, but I never caught up with Sully. I could hear yelling and branches breaking ahead of me, but the forest was too thick to see him.

The jet engine changed pitch again: it was winding up.

"No, no, no, no, no."

But my chanting made no difference. The rotors drummed harder and harder until the sound was moving again. It had taken off and, if my sense of direction was right for once, it was flying low and out to sea.

I tripped and came down onto the soft sand. It knocked the wind out of me, but it wasn't the fall that brought the tears to my eyes. It was the whole stupid frustration of being late for a train, but the train wasn't a train, it was a helicopter and it wasn't taking us into the city so we could go to the museum – it was the thing that was going to save our lives. I lay there, spitting sand and sobbing, until I heard Sully shouting.

The ant-people.

I was on my feet and running again. There was nothing left in me, but I ran and ran until I was on the wide white beach of Whalers Cove. It was low tide. There were footprints everywhere in the sand – big boots and bare feet all on top of each other. They'd been made after the rain had washed the sand smooth, but the people who'd made them were long gone.

Sully was twenty metres up the beach on his knees, his face in his hands. I could hear him crying from where I stood, but I didn't go to him. I flopped on my butt and felt my lungs puffing out the last of my hope. I couldn't believe it. I almost laughed. We finally make it to the place we'd been fighting to find for two days and everybody had gone. No note left for us – only the laminated page about the whale carcass. Not even anything scratched in the sand.

I dragged myself to the campsite, but everything had gone – even my pack and the tent I was supposed to share with David had gone. The campsite was so clean, I had to wonder if any kids had ever camped there. Maybe this was the next sick chapter in the nightmare of my life? Maybe it had all been a dream and I was really stuck in some hospital bed somewhere in a coma, and all this awfulness was just imagining?

I found a tent peg and a butter knife with a snapped blade. I spotted a chocolate wrapper under a fern and I wondered if Rachael had raided Bethany's pack after all. It'd be like she'd stolen jewellery from the dead if she had.

I zombied around the campsite in a state of utter disbelief for a good half-hour. Nobody jumped out of the bushes shouting, "Surprise!" There was no stash of food left for us. They must have given up. Even my parents must have given up. Two days of looking and they call it quits? *Two days*? Is *that* all we're worth?

It started raining. It was a light drizzle but it made me curse. I wanted to get all dramatic and shout "Why?" at the heavens but, with my face pointing skywards, the tiny pinpricks felt good on my cheeks and eyelids. The irony and the hopelessness got the better of me and I started laughing. It was either that or start crying like Sully.

When the drizzle and the dumb laughing fit passed and my heart was no longer beating in my temples, I realised the girls had taken a very long time. That was when I heard the whistling over the dull shhh of the cove. Then one of Emily's ear-piercing shrieks that sent me scurrying back up the track.

Chapter Seventeen

They hadn't made it far. Emily was sitting on the track with her legs stretched out. Bethany was at her side, curled up in a ball like an unborn baby. Emily had one hand on Bethany's shoulder. I could hear her crying.

"Are they there?" Emily asked. "Did you make it?"

I shook my head.

She cursed, grabbed a handful of sand and pelted it at the ferns.

Bethany turned up the volume.

"What happened?"

"She tripped and fell. With me on her back. She hurt her leg."

We helped her sit up. There was a cut on her left knee.

"Ouch," Emily said. "That looks nasty."

"Come on. We'll help you down to the beach so

you can wash it clean."

I dragged the sniffing Bethany to her feet, then helped Emily stand, and together the three of us – me in the middle with a wounded soldier on each arm – hobbled to the cove.

Sully's eyes were raw, though he had stopped crying.

"Oh, great! Another injury. Now how are we supposed to get out of here?" His voice was shaky. He had his arms crossed tightly against his chest.

I'd been thinking the same thing. We could carry one passenger each, though Bethany weighed more than Emily. My fuel tank was on empty – had been for a day or so. Sully had surprised me with his endurance, but I doubted he'd be in any better condition to play horse.

"We wait," I said. "They'll be back."

"How can you be so sure?" Bethany said. "What if that was the last of them?"

"Do you think your mum would stop looking after only two nights?" I asked. After the shock of the cove being empty had passed, I knew they would still be looking. They were just looking in the wrong place.

Bethany shook her head. "Of course not. She'll be out there with my stepdad. Somewhere."

"Mine, too," Emily said.

"My stepdad couldn't give a stuff." Sully spat as he spoke. "He'll be home watching TV. He'll know we've been found when they say it on the news."

We looked at him, waiting for the smile that made it all a joke, but it never came.

"That's crap, Sully," Bethany said. "And you know it. He has his own problems, but he'll be looking for you, I know."

Sully scoffed and looked along the beach.

"What about your mum?" Emily asked him.

Bethany grabbed at her pants and mouthed "No!" but it was too late – the question had been asked.

"Mum doesn't live with us any more."

There was a long silence – as if that had really been a bomb going off and my ears hadn't recovered.

"I'm . . . sorry. I didn't realise."

He shrugged. "I don't go around telling everyone the details of my train wreck of a life. I'd prefer it if you didn't, either. That's if we ever make it out of here."

"Of course," Emily said.

I nodded in agreement, but I wanted to know more. I wanted to know what happened. I wanted to know if she was ever coming home, but I wasn't going to ask.

"That's why I'm staying with you guys," he said and sniffed. "You'll have people looking for you and, if you get found, then I will, too."

That was sad. I kept searching his face for a smile that would turn it into irony, but there was nothing there. He believed what he said. In that one minute I had learned more about Sully than I had in all the years we'd been at school together, and hearing the truth about his life made his attitude and his determination make sense. He didn't seem like such a self-centred idiot now that I knew there was a reason for it. I'd treat him differently from that moment on, even if I tried not to.

I put my hand on his shoulder. "Thanks for sticking with us. We wouldn't have made it without you."

He smiled then. It was just a little flashing curl of the lip, but it was a smile. "Probably wouldn't have got lost in the first place, either, if I hadn't been there."

"Crap," Emily said. "That was a team effort!"

A thick column of sunlight raced along the cove and bathed us in very welcome warmth. We squinted and moaned our delight. I felt as if I hadn't seen the sun in days . . . probably because I *hadn't*!

"Now what?" Sully said.

"Now we make ourselves comfortable," I said. "Beds for the cripples. Food."

"I'll have a pie," Sully grumbled. "With sauce."

"Done," I said. "Any other orders?"

"Pie for me, too, please," Bethany said. "No sauce though."

"Em?"

"I'm right at the moment," she said, rubbing her belly. "Still full from a couple of days ago. Though if you happen to see any of those wild boars you were talking about, I'll have six. Actually, better make it seven."

"Right, ten wild boars and two pies, one with sauce. I'll see what I can do."

Chapter Eighteen

I must be solar-powered. The more the sun shone, the better I felt. Sully helped the girls up to the driest sand at the top of the beach and literally made them beds of long fern fronds.

I walked the beach but found nothing that resembled food – though I admit I did look twice at the whale carcass. When I made it downwind of the thing, I knew *for certain* that it was way too long dead to be human food. I saw schools of tiny fish in the waves but had no idea how to catch them without a net. Or cook them without a fire.

I had another look at the campsite and it was the broken butter knife that gave me the idea. The butter knife and *Asterix*. The other thing that Obelix loves to eat, besides wild boar, grows on the rocks on the coast near his little Gaulish village. They also grew on the rocks in Whalers Cove.

Oysters.

I took my shoes and socks and shirt off, but left my pants on and stashed the broken knife in my pocket. I waved to the crew up the beach and kicked through the small waves and into the bay.

"What are you doing, idiot?" Bethany squealed.

I dived. The water was bearably cold and felt oh so stingy-nice on my bush-battered skin. I swam across the cove and whooped out loud when I realised there were literally hundreds of big, fat oysters on the rocks.

The low tide meant I had places to stand and I used the broken knife to chip the biggest and best ones off their stony homes. When I accidentally smashed one in half, revealing the slimy little animal inside, I gouged it out in one piece, picking off the fragments of shell. Then I closed my eyes and swallowed the thing. It slid down my throat and into the hollow chamber of my stomach with ease. All that was left in my mouth was a pleasantly salty fishiness . . . and a bit of shell grit.

I accidentally smashed (and ate) another six before my pockets were full and I'd honestly never enjoyed a meal of raw seafood more. That was mostly because I'd never eaten raw seafood of any kind before, but it wasn't as bad as it sounded. When

Sully saw what I was emptying from my bulging wet pockets, his eyes lit up.

"Oysters! Man, I love oysters. Oysters Kilpatrick, oh yeah!"

I collected a rock from the campsite for a table and set about gouging the shellfish open with the broken knife. The guys watched intently.

"Oh, I'm not eating that," Bethany said. "Aren't they poisonous? I'm not *that* hungry. I'll never be *that* hungry."

I picked the first one clean and handed it in half of its shell to Emily.

Her eyes grew wide and her mouth turned down at the edges.

"They're good," I said. "Best thing I've eaten in a couple of days."

She took it with a chuckle and sucked the oyster meat down with a slurp, then shut her eyes and swallowed hard. When she looked up again, her eyes were smiling.

She nodded slowly. "Not bad," she said. "I'd do that again."

I opened one for Sully and he didn't hesitate. He gulped it down, gagged, shivered and coughed.

"Beautiful," he moaned. He wiped his lips then took a big swig from Emily's water bottle.

"You found water?"

Sully nodded. "There's a little stream behind the campsite."

It was tea-stained brown, but it tasted okay.

"Give us another one of those slimy beasts," he said. "Pity we have nothing to cook them on."

The next shell came apart perfectly and I offered it to Bethany. She shook her head but, when I went to give it to Sully instead, she stopped me.

"Okay, okay. I'll try it," she said. "But, if I spew up, I'm going to spew on you."

"Charming," I said.

She didn't spew. She ate another. And another. She still didn't spew.

Chapter Nineteen

Sully swam out with me the second time. We loaded our pockets until we could barely swim and ate until we couldn't eat any more. With our withered bellies full, we stretched out in the sun and, one by one, grew still and slept.

I woke to the sting of a March fly biting my foot. I slapped it hard and buried its broken corpse in the sand with my toes.

"Sorry. I couldn't reach that one," Emily said. She was sitting beside me with my T-shirt in her hand, smiling. She waved the shirt at another flying beast that was looking for a landing spot on my back.

I sat up and blinked at the brightness of the day. The sun was high. Hours had passed.

I scanned the beach. "No signs of life?"

"Nothing."

She nodded her head at the sleeping couple

beside us. They were holding hands.

I looked at Emily, puzzled.

She shrugged. "Crazy little thing called love."

I shook my head in disbelief.

She shifted and winced.

"How's your ankle?"

"Hurts like nothing else."

I took a closer look. She'd taken her boot and sock off and her ankle looked like it was about to give birth to twins. Big, purple twin ankles.

"Ouch!" I said.

"It's not bad if I can keep the weight off it. I don't think it's broken."

I wriggled closer and kissed her bulging ankle as gently as I could.

"Thanks. Feels better already."

She shut her eyes and tilted her head toward the sun. I took her hand and she squeezed gently. I squeezed back then turned my own face to the sun.

Beside us, Bethany stirred and moaned and we dropped hands. It was a secret too new and fragile to be shared with anyone, let alone Bethany.

If only we could have wiped the smiles off our faces.

"Look at you two," Bethany said, sitting up. "What have you been up to while I was sleeping?"

"Nothing," Emily said.

"Just soaking up the sun," I said.

Bethany scoffed. "Is that what you call it?"

"What do *you* call it?" Emily said, pointing at Sully.

She'd let his hand go and now she snorted with contempt. "It's never going to happen."

"Why not? You guys fight like you're married."

"Exactly," she said. She cupped her hand around her mouth and whispered. "Trust me, Sully's pain is a whole lot bigger than he lets on."

"But surely . . ." Emily began.

"My mum's in jail," Sully said into the sand. He sat up. "She didn't pay her fines. She's so pig-headed. They mounted up and up and then she *couldn't* pay her fines, so they locked her up."

Bethany looked at him with her mouth open. Eventually, she patted his shoulder. "You're having a big day today, Sully. Spilling all your big, dark secrets."

His mum was in jail? In jail for being pig-headed? Like mother, like son, I thought and almost made myself laugh.

"Isn't that what you're supposed to do before you die?" Sully said. "Anyway, it's not as if you hadn't told anybody."

"I hadn't!" Bethany said, suddenly angry. "I did not tell a soul. Not a single person. That's one secret *you'll* have to tell the world."

"And he just did," Emily said.

So I'd heard right. Jye Sullivan, the guy who'd tormented my whole world since primary school, had just revealed that his mother was in prison. That was a big thing. It was bigger than being lost. It was bigger than being eaten alive by insects and nearly freezing to death. It was bigger than hunger and missing our rescuers by mere minutes.

"Yes," Bethany said. "You told me you were never going to tell anybody about that."

Sully put his hands behind his head and flopped back on the sand. "Bound to come out sooner or later. Not my fault. Besides, these guys are trustworthy. Aren't you?"

"Of course," Emily said and nudged me.

"So your mum doesn't live with you," I said. "Because she's in jail. Any other secret landmines you'd like to set off before you die?"

"He's not going to die," Emily said. "Nobody's going to die. They *will* find us."

"I know that," Sully mumbled.

"Then why all the famous last words?" Bethany asked.

"I don't know," he said. "It's being out here. It's being lost. Makes you realise what's important and what's not."

Emily looked at me. I had to agree with him on that one. The truth serum of being lost in the wilderness was bubbling in my veins, too.

"Even after all the crap I've dumped on Kingy . . . for *years* I've been paying out on him. Since primary school."

I nodded and smiled.

"Yeah, you know it. Even after all that crap, when I was out of my head . . . cold and lost and . . . freaking out, he gave me a hug like he was . . . my mum or something."

"I didn't see that," Bethany said.

"Don't know how you missed it," Sully said. "You were right there."

"Oh, so I was!" Bethany said. She giggled. "I was hanging on the other side of him! It was dark. I couldn't see."

"It doesn't matter how messed up your life is – and I think you'd have to agree that mine needs more than a new set of tyres and an oil change – that stuff *means* something."

I squirmed. I didn't like where this was going. I mean, I liked the fact that it meant something that I hugged him . . . but what did it mean exactly?

"Don't get me wrong," Sully said. "I'm not asking you to join the family. I just think you're a much bigger dude than I ever gave you credit for. If it'd been you freaking out instead of me, I don't know if I would have had the guts to . . . you know . . ."

"You're freaking *me* out now, Sully," Bethany said, spooked. "I've never heard you say so many nice . . . intelligent . . . kind things about anybody."

"Well, it's not just Kingy. His girlfriend played the part of mum the night before. Thanks, Emily."

Emily blushed and nodded. "No worries."

"What about me?" Bethany moaned.

He took her hand and kissed it. "You know I love you. I'm just messed up."

She snatched her hand back playfully. "Keep away from me, stranger."

"Charming," Emily and I said at the same time.

Chapter Twenty

We swam over and got more oysters in the late afternoon. The tide had changed and we had to dive for them. Sully hadn't changed, but I saw him very differently. The more details I knew about his life, the more sense he made. I had a feeling that, even when he knew exactly where he was in the world – in the lounge or the PE hall – he'd still be lost inside. But he could swim like a dolphin. He nearly caught a fish – he scooped it out of the water, but it flipped once and was gone. God knows what we would have done with it if he'd landed it.

We thawed on the rocks before heading back.

"We could live out here, you know," he said.

"Not very comfortably, but yes."

"No, with a tent and a stove and a spear and a net. We could do it."

I nodded. "I'd miss my tuba."

He laughed. "And I'd miss my slot-car set."

I looked at him sideways.

"Don't tell anybody. Ever. Or I'll have to kill you."

I licked the salty water off my finger and crossed my heart. "Promise."

Our rescuer didn't fall from the sky. There was no megaphone or bright flares or being hoisted aloft on wire rope. Our rescuer was a hairy ranger on a four-wheeled motorbike.

"Ohhh," Sully moaned. "We don't even get a ride in a helicopter. I want my money back!"

"I think you might be the guys we've been looking for," the man said through his bushy beard. "What do you reckon?"

Sully walked straight up to the bloke and hugged him around the neck. The bloke – who later introduced himself as Steve – patted Sully's back and grinned. Bethany and Emily sounded like puppies in the pound. And, yes, my eyes did water and, yes, there were tears . . . so, yes . . . I did cry.

Nothing like my mum did though.

Steve radioed ahead, then carried us back to the car park one by one. Emily, Bethany, Sully, then me.

It felt like there were a hundred people there to

greet us. People I didn't know, many of them dressed in bright orange coveralls – police, an ambulance with three officers and the whole outdoor education class, including Pearson and Mrs Kennedy. And there was Mum and Dad and Matty, all bawling their eyes out and looking like they'd slept even less than I had. I hugged anybody who got too close. Everybody was talking at once.

"We were looking in the wrong place," Matty said.

"Somebody found a hat they thought belonged to Jye Sullivan up on the west side of Mount Vereker," Dad shouted.

"Then someone found a watch and an empty water bottle. We thought we were getting close," Mum said, right in my ear. She wouldn't let me go, but I didn't care. "How wrong could we be? Oh, you're safe. You're SAFE!"

She hugged me tighter and wet my cheek with her tears.

An ambulance officer wearing disposable blue gloves muscled through the crowd and checked me over. He asked me a hundred questions, but he was smiling and only half-listening to my answers. He patted my head and told me I was okay.

Then a lady wearing make-up with big hair and

a nice suit pushed her way to the front of the crowd. She held a microphone and had the strangest lopsided smile I'd ever seen. The bloke behind her carried a video camera and she introduced herself as such-and-such from something-or-other news. She babbled at me and I nodded blindly until a light on the camera came on and she spoke into the microphone.

"We're here with one of the lucky survivors. Two nights lost in the wilderness. Peter King, how are you feeling?"

I couldn't stop smiling. "A bit tired. Hungry. Anybody got a spare sandwich?"

There was laughter, then someone did hand me a tomato and cheese sandwich.

I took a bite. "It's good!"

More laughter.

"How did you do it?" the reporter asked. "We've had some cold and unfriendly weather over the last few days."

I shrugged. "We just stuck together."

"And what did you eat? Nothing? For almost three days?"

"Oysters," I said, and licked my lips. "Today we lazed around in the sun and ate oysters."

"Raw?"

"Is there any other way?"

There was a chorus of eeeeews from the crowd and then the reporter was congratulating me again and saying goodbye.

Sully pushed through the bodies. He looked distressed. "They're taking Em. In the ambulance."

"Is she okay?"

"Yeah. She said she wanted to see you."

I gave my sandwich to Mum and shoved through the crowd. Hands patted my back, faces I knew and many I didn't.

"Well done," they said. "Welcome back."

I found the ambulance, with Emily sitting up in the back. She saw me, heaved a massive sigh and beckoned me on board. The ambulance officer who'd checked me out stepped aside so I could climb on.

Emily hugged me and kissed my cheek. She introduced her mum, Cassandra, and her dad, Keith. Her mum hugged me and thanked me. Her dad shook my hand and patted my back. He was still in his policeman's uniform, though it was a bit the worse for wear. "Well done, Peter. Thanks for looking after our Emmy."

I huffed. "She was looking after me most of the time."

Emily's face was scratched, dirty and a little bit sad. I knew what she was feeling. I could read it in her eyes. I was feeling it, too. All the people, all the fuss. I just wanted *them* to get lost.

"We're about to move out," the ambulance guy said.

I kissed Emily and waved as they closed the door and drove off.

Bethany was waiting. She hugged me around the neck until my face was red, then introduced me to her mum and stepdad, but it was all just noise. The ambulance officer had treated the cut on her knee and bandaged it. She let herself be helped to the waiting four-wheel drive and blew me a kiss as they left.

Sully was sitting on a low wooden sign next to a man in a white T-shirt, his arms and neck blue with old tattoos. Sully nodded to me and smiled. He introduced me to his stepdad, Rhys, who shook my hand and looked right into my eyes.

"Thanks for looking after my boy," he said. His voice was grumbly and warm.

"Team effort," I said.

Sully stood and we hugged. A big, brave, friendly hug that went on forever.

"Thanks," he said.

"Thank *you*."

"If you ever need an orienteering partner, you know who *not* to choose."

"Bah," I said. "You'll be at the top of my list."

He laughed and it came out all squeal-soaked and silly.

"I like a bit of adventure."

Chapter Twenty-one

At the end of every *Asterix* book, the inhabitants of the little Gaulish village have a banquet under the stars. They eat roast boar around a huge fire and everybody's happy – everybody except the bard, who is gagged and bound to a tree because his singing is so bad, a few notes from one of his ballads makes it rain.

My banquet was roast *lamb* with vegetables and the warmth I felt was a direct result of the bath Dad ran for me. Oh, man, that was the best bath in history. With my head back and my ears covered with water, I couldn't hear the TV in the lounge, but I could hear my heart beating.

I realised that Mum had been right about the outdoor education camp: it *was* good for me. Better than any class I'd ever had. Taught me more about my place in the world in two days than I'd learned in years of stuffy classrooms.

Being lost can be a scary thing. But sometimes, when you get lost, you also find out what's real.